SULLIVAN

LAUREL SPRINGS EMERGENCY RESPONSE TEAM #5

LARAMIE BRISCOE

Copyright © 2020 Laramie Briscoe

All rights reserved. No part of this book may be reproduced, transmitted, downloaded, distributed, stored in or introduced into any information storage and retrieval system, in any form or by any means, whether electronic or mechanical, without express permission of the author, except by a reviewer who may quote brief passages for review purposes.

This book is a work of fiction and any resemblance to any person, living or dead, or any events or occurrences, is purely coincidental. The characters and storylines are created from the author's imagination or are used fictitiously. Any trademarks, service marks, product names, or named features are assumed to be the property of their respective owners, and are used only for reference. There is no implied endorsement if any of these terms are used. Except for review purposes, the reproduction of this book in whole or part, electronically or mechanically, constitutes a copyright violation.

Editor: Elfwerks Editing

Beta Readers: Danielle Wentworth

Proofreader: Danielle Wentworth

Cover: Laramie Briscoe

Cover Photography: Wander Aguiar

Formatting: Laramie Briscoe

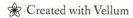 Created with Vellum

ALSO BY LARAMIE BRISCOE

The Haldonia Monarchy

Royal Rebel

Royal Chaos

Royal Love

Heaven Hill Series

Meant To Be

Out of Darkness

Losing Control

Worth The Battle

Dirty Little Secret

Second Chance Love

Rough Patch

Beginning of Forever

Home Free

Shield My Heart

A Heaven Hill Christmas

Heaven Hill Next Generation

Hurricane

Wild

Fury

Hollow

Restraint

Heaven Hill Shorts

Caelin

Christine

Justice

Harley

Jagger

Charity

Liam

Drew

Dalton

Mandy

Rockin' Country Series

Only The Beginning

The Price of Love

Full Circle

Hard To Love

Reaper's Love

The Nashvegas Trilogy

Power Couple

Breach of Contract

The Moonshine Task Force Series

Renegade

Tank

Havoc

Ace

Menace

Cruise

Laurel Springs Emergency Response Team

Ransom

Suppression

Enigma

Cutter

Sullivan

Devante

The MVP Duet

On the DL

MVP

The Midnight Cove Series

Inflame

Stand Alones

My Confession

Sketch

Sass

Trick

Room 143

2018 Laramie Briscoe Compilation

2019 Laramie Briscoe Compilation

NEW RELEASE ALERTS

JOIN MY MAILING LIST
http://sitel.ink/LBList

JOIN MY READERS GROUP
fbl.ink/LaramiesLounge

TEXT LARAMIE TO 88202

MOONSHINE TASK FORCE MEMBERS

Ryan "Renegade" Kepler – Married to Whitney and father to Stella and Nick. Best friend to Trevor.

Trevor "Tank" Trumboldt – Married to Blaze, brother to Whitney, uncle to Stella and Nick. Best friend to Ryan.

Holden "Havoc" Thompson – Married to Leighton, father to Ransom and Cutter. Best friend to Mason.

Anthony "Ace" Bailey – Married to Violet.

Mason "Menace" Harrison – Married to Karina, father to Caleb and Kelsea, grandfather to Molly and Levi. Best friend to Holden.

Caleb "Cruise" Harrison – Married to Ruby, father to Molly and Levi, son of Mason, brother to Kelsea.

BLURB

Sullivan Baker

Moving to Laurel Springs and joining the LSERT was the best spur-of-the-moment decision I ever made. Here, out from under the expectations of my Police Chief father, I'm thriving.

I've found a boldness and confidence I never had in Paradise Lost.

And a woman who I can't stop thinking or dreaming about, and don't want to stay away from. Attorney Shelby Bruce knocked me for a loop and my head hasn't stopped spinning since the night of our "friendmas" Christmas party.

When there's a physical threat to her wellbeing, I won't stop at anything to protect her, even if it means losing a piece of myself in the process.

Shelby Bruce

Houston was my home until the big city reached out and bit me. Laurel Springs is more my speed, and I've settled into life here.

A new friend group, building my practice from the

ground up, and a smoking hot new love interest have my life extremely busy and full. I'm content. More so than I ever was in my *old existence*.

That all changes when I revise a will for one of the pillars of the Laurel Springs community. Effectively, she cuts her grandson out of her fortune. When he finds out it's not pretty.

Even worse. He blames me.

But something amazing happens. Day by day, I realize the relationships I've built within the community and the LSERT are stronger than I ever imagined. Especially when Sullivan Baker saves not only my life, but my heart.

PROLOGUE
SULLIVAN

"YES!"

My sister screams the word as she tackles her boyfriend to the ground. He's proposed in front of what has become our group of friends, and though I feel a stab of jealousy in my chest, I'm excited for them. I can't help but clap and whistle along with everyone else.

Cutter and I talked about this a few days ago. He asked my dad, but he requested my permission too, knowing how close Rowan and I are.

I gave it to him with every single blessing I could muster. If anyone deserves to be happy, it's Rowan. Someone taps on my shoulder, causing me to take my eyes off the ecstatic couple.

"Is it possible to be that lucky? To get someone who makes you smile and your eyes twinkle?"

Attorney Shelby Bruce has had my attention since I moved here a few months ago. We live in the same apartment complex, and she just so happens to take her morning run either when I'm leaving for or coming home from work.

She may be a bit of an obsession. One I wish I had time to explore.

"According to them, it most definitely is."

She snorts loudly, bringing her glass of what smells like Jack and Coke up to her mouth. Instead of a small sip, she chugs almost half the container, licking the residue from her lips when she pulls it back. Now that I look at her, I realize she's had a few.

"You doing alright?"

Her smile is lopsided. "Better than I have in a long time."

My sister chooses that moment to run at me, throwing herself into my arms, effectively cutting off the conversation Shelby and I are having. Instead of sticking around, the object of my affection strolls across the room.

"Did you know?" Her eyes are wet with tears, but this time is different from all the other times I've seen them fall down her face. These are joyous.

"I did, I'm so happy for you, Ro."

She hugs me tightly. "You're gonna get this too." Her words are slightly muffled by my t-shirt. "I just know it."

"I know."

The words sound weak, but there's nothing I will do to dampen the excitement of this moment for her.

"Hey." Cutter gets my attention, holding his hand out.

"Congratulations, man, I'm happy for y'all." We shake, a mutual respect flowing between the two of us.

"Thank you, I appreciate you giving me your blessing."

"You didn't need it."

"But I wanted it."

And that's why there's such respect between the two of us.

"It's no big deal."

He runs a hand through his hair, resting it on the back of his neck. "So I kinda have another favor to ask you. Shelby's a little toasted, you think you can make sure she gets home okay?"

I've done my best to ignore her because I hate that I want to be around her all the time, to get to know her, but I'm unsure of how she would take it. Sighing, I look from one side of the room to the other and find her green eyes on me.

Eating. Me. Up.

Raising an eyebrow at her, I brush Cutter away and take myself over to where she stands in the corner.

"You okay, Shelby?"

"You seem to ask me that a lot, Sully." She leans in. "What if I told you, you could make it all okay?"

"I'd say it's probably time to take you home."

"Is it?"

"Yeah, yeah it is."

"DO you mind if I roll down the window?"

"It's December, but go right ahead," I chuckle as she fumbles with the buttons on the door. "Here." I use the main control on my side. "How far do you want it?"

She looks back at me, smiling like a little nymph. "As far as it can go."

Fuck. Me.

We're quiet as I drive us to our apartment building, neither of us saying much, but there's a string of chemistry between us. Like always, it's vibrating with unexplored need. I'm amped up, I feel like I'm about to go into a building with unknown occupants and an undetermined amount of guns. My adrenaline is spiking hardcore for her.

Pulling into my assigned parking space, I shut my Mustang off before looking over at her. The lights from the dash cast a low glow around us. "I got you here safely."

"So you did." She fumbles with her seatbelt, her shoulder-length hair moving so that I can't see her face, but there's a touch of disappointment in her tone. "Thanks for the ride."

"Somehow I don't think I gave you the ride you wanted."

She stops what she's doing, inhaling deeply. "You wouldn't know, you never asked."

Those words punch me hard in the gut, because I don't believe for a second that's what she's saying to me. Reaching up, I rub against the stubble on my chin, taking a deep breath to calm myself down.

"So what are you thinking?" I chuckle. "One night stand? Friends with benefits?"

"Why do we have to put a label on it? Why can't we do what feels good? Why do we have to make decisions right this instant?" She seems irritated with answering questions, even though she's the one asking them. It gives me more insight into her frame of mind than she even understands.

"You know what I think, Counselor?"

She slings her hair out of the way, giving me her eyes again. Hers travel up to mine, eyebrow lifting in question.

"I think you have so much control in the courtroom, you want someone to take control in your personal life, I mean…" I lean in closer, propping my elbow up on the center console. "Correct me if I'm wrong."

She doesn't move, all she does is close her eyes. "You're not wrong." The words are so soft I almost don't hear them.

"Is this *drunk Shelby* talking? Or is this the *Shelby who hides everything she wants* talking?"

Her green eyes shine in the muted tone of the security light shining down from above this parking spot. "This is the Shelby who hides everything she truly wants. The one who has to look professional all the time, the one who always has it together, who always has the answer for every fuckin' question people ask."

My mouth and lips are dry as fuck, I get what she's putting down.

"Want me to walk you up to your apartment?"

She lives two floors up from me, and immediately I see the disappointment in her eyes as she avoids my gaze.

"Or do you want to come to mine?"

A small smile spreads across her face. "Mine," she whispers.

"Sit tight."

Getting out and shutting the driver's door, I take a moment to adjust my dick. It got fifteen times harder than it's ever been. Calm down, my brain tells the rod in between my legs.

When I get over to her side of the car, I open the door for her. She turns, spreading her thighs for me.

"Promise me, Sully." Her voice is soft. "Promise this doesn't change our friendship."

This is going to completely change our friendship, but I give her the answer she wants. "We're good, no matter what happens here, tonight."

My hands go around her waist, pulling her out, making sure she's on solid ground before grabbing her fingers, leading us up the steps. As I pass my apartment, there's a part of me that screams to go in there and not do what I'm about to. Laying my heart out isn't something I've done easily since we lost Etta. Honestly, she's the last person I gave my love to so easily.

I shut that shit down real quick.

The closer we get to her front door, the harder my heart beats.

She fumbles with her keys, so I end up taking them out of her hand and opening the door for her. I've been in here a few times, but now isn't the moment I want to comment on her decorating ability.

"So." I shove my hands in the pockets of my jeans, rocking back on my feet. "Should we just go for it or, is there something specific you're expecting." The last thing I want to do is ruin our friendship or change the dynamic of our friend group.

She giggles, throaty and deep. "I leave it up to you, Sully. Give me what you do best."

She wants what I do best? Then that's what she'll fucking get.

Looking around the apartment, I see exactly what I'm going to use. One of the two chairs she has at her kitchen table. Grabbing her by the hand, I pull her over.

"My kitchen?" Her eyes are clouded with question.

"You'll see," I say the words like the promise they are.

She's tall, especially in her high-heeled boots, and I appreciate not having to bend at the waist to take what I want. I put my arm behind her neck, grasping, pulling her closer to me. It knocks her off-balance slightly, and when I take her lips it's on a small gasp.

Her open mouth allows my tongue to go right for what I want, brushing the roof in a possession I've needed to have since the first day I saw her running.

She grabs for me, using her fingers digging into my biceps to hold her up.

But when I've had my fill for the moment, I gently direct her to the chair, before walking around behind her, grabbing hold of her arms.

"Sully?"

"You trust me, right?" My voice is tight with desire, heavy with need for her.

"Yeah, I trust you with everything." She looks at me, over her shoulder. "I'm a pretty good judge of character."

"That right?" I grin.

"That's right."

When I have her arms behind the chair, I reach for a pair of cuffs I carry at the small of my back, just in case they're ever needed. I slap them on, locking them, but making sure she has plenty of room.

"Sullivan, did you just handcuff me to this chair?"

Nosing her hair out of the way, I get to her ear. "Sure did. You okay with that, Counselor?"

The length of her quietness almost makes me take them off, but when I'm just about to do it, I hear her answer. Strong and loud. "Perfectly..."

Reaching around her, I place my hands on her chest, allowing her to get used to the feel of them against her. Quickly, she tilts her head back, resting it flush against my chest, which gives me the perfect angle to lean down and fuse our lips together again.

This kiss? It's a sensual exploration coupled with a slow fuck between our tongues. It might have lasted two minutes or two hours, all I know is when I pull away, we're both panting, affected by what's going on here.

Cautiously I drop my hands to cup her breasts, just to

see how she responds. When she presses them harder into my palms, I know she's down for my plans. Coming around to her front, I grab the other chair and have a seat, so that we're almost at eye level with one another.

Leaning forward, I capture one of her hard nipples, nipping slightly against the cotton of her shirt and the material of her bra.

She makes a frustrated sound in her through. "I want this off," she pulls at the cuffs around her hands.

"Do you love this shirt?" I ask the question with a raised eyebrow.

"Why are you asking me this right now? It's not a favorite if that's what you want to know."

I slightly shift to the side, reaching into my boots to grab a knife I keep there. I open it.

"Don't move," I caution her as I slip it into the neckline, the fabric slicing cleanly.

She gasps, her eyes wide with what appear to be wonder. There's not a doubt she likes this. Shelby seems to have a bit of the same side I have, and if we can explore it together, then all the better for it.

What's before me is more than I ever imagined. Her breasts are larger than I thought, barely held in by the lace cups shielding them from my gaze. Tilting my head to the side, I give them a good look, dropping my eyes to where her jeans button at her waist.

Reaching forward, I pull one of the cups down as far as I can. It's not far enough to get access to the flesh, though.

"Take it off," she moans.

Because her hands are still cuffed, it's not that easy. Flipping my knife open again, I place it in the middle of her chest. "Seriously don't move this time."

"I trust you," she whispers.

With a flick of the wrist, I slice through the fabric, leaving it gaping open. Her chest is jutted out because of the position she's in, and before I take her hardened nipple with my mouth, I place the blunt edge of the knife against the peaked nub and rub it down in a swift motion.

Shelby jerks slightly, her eyes dilating as they watch what I'm doing.

Once they're hard enough to my liking, I lean forward, taking her nipple in my mouth, tonguing at the pebbled flesh, nipping and kissing.

My hands move down her body, stopping at the closure of her jeans, before unbuttoning it, and quickly taking them off. Her panties are wet in the middle, just how I wanted them to be. Pulling back from her tits, I ask, "You want me?"

Her blonde hair falls into her eyes as she nods, tilting her head back against her shoulders. "Please, please," she begs thrusting up to me. "I'm so empty."

What I wouldn't give to slide my dick deep into that pussy, but I don't have protection, and this isn't the type of woman you go raw in on the first date. But this is more about her, than it ever was about me. Instead, I take two fingers, stick them in my mouth, swirl my tongue to make sure they're nice and lubricated before removing them and thrusting them into her core.

She clamps down hard enough to almost make me come in my jeans.

"Sully," she screams as I feel her tight channel gripping me.

"You okay, Counselor?" I wipe my fingers on my jeans, before looking up at her.

Those green eyes of hers are closed, and her head is

tilted to the side, her lips parted slightly as she breathes a rhythm sending her chest up and down. A laugh rumbles up into my throat, and I give myself a couple of minutes to get my shit together.

Once I do, I get up, un-cuff Shelby and pick her up. Even though I've been here a few times, I've never been to her bedroom, but luckily for me, her apartment is the exact same layout as mine.

Her blankets are already pulled back, I lay her down, take her shoes off, get rid of the clothing hanging from her arms, and cover her up.

For a woman who always looks so fierce and put together in everyday life, she resembles a teenager in sleep. I can't help but lean over and place a kiss on her forehead.

"Sleep good, Counselor."

I lock up, and exit. Outside, I run my fingers through my hair wondering what in the hell has just gone on between us.

And, when will it happen again?

CHAPTER 1
SHELBY

MY HAND TREMBLES as I stand outside Sully's apartment. I know he's off-shift, both his cruiser and Mustang are parked next to one another. I'm holding a roast in my other palm, nervous as hell. Lifting up the trembling hand, I knock quickly on the door, inwardly dying as I wait for him to either answer or come to the door.

"Coming." I hear his strong voice through the barrier between us. When he opens it, I literally lose my breath.

"Counselor." He grins as he sees me standing there.

"Hey," I answer. "I made a huge dinner, and was wondering if you wanted to split it with me."

He rubs his stomach, inadvertently lifting his shirt up so I can see his abdomen muscles. It's an unconscious move he makes, but I still let my gaze drift down and enjoy the fruits of his exercise labor.

"Whatever that is smells amazing, c'mon in."

Ducking under his arm, I enter, feeling shy because this is one of the first times we've seen each other since the

Christmas party. It's not that I've avoided him, I've just waited for him to make a move.

He hasn't.

Which is why I'm here tonight. To try and figure out if I can convince myself to be bold again.

Going over to the island, I put everything down, starting to unpack it.

"What did you bring?"

He has a seat in one of the chairs, looking at me expectantly.

"Top round was on sale at the grocery store and I couldn't pass it up, it's way too much for just me though."

I'm rambling and I know it, but I can't seem to stop. The last time we were alone together he rubbed a knife against my nipple for God sake's.

"I don't wanna eat all your food." He seems maybe almost as awkward as I am after what happened between the two of us.

"This is only half of it, believe it or not."

His eyes bulge as he sees the Dutch oven I have almost full to the brim. "No shit?"

The uttered words cause me to laugh. "No shit. I hope you like slightly spicy though. I put pepperoncini's in it."

"Never had it before, but I'm up for anything."

I grin, happy to share with him. Excited to be in the same space together. Hoping like hell we'll be able to move forward from what went on in my apartment. Putting the bag I have shouldered on the island, I pull out rice and corn bread too, along with a big piece of chocolate cake. "Kinda went all out."

"I can see that." His eyes are huge, but his stomach growls loudly. "Have to admit, I'm not sorry you did."

"Let me get us some plates."

I've been here enough times that I know where things are. I'm comfortable in a way I haven't ever been with anyone else, but I don't know how to approach the subject of us being together. In a perfect world, he would take control of this, just like I asked him to that night, but Sullivan is a gentleman. Unless he's told not to be.

Can I do that?

Will I ever be as bold as I was that night?

I'm not sure I can be, but I want more than anything to be the woman he comes home to. The one he lets that side of himself out with, and the lover he calls in the middle of the night when he needs relief. So I know I have to somehow figure out what I want to do, which is why I lunge forward. "The Christmas party was fun, huh?"

Putting a plate piled high with food in front of him is a way for me to hide my embarrassment.

"Yeah, it was. Glad I could get you safely into your apartment." He takes a bite. "You were pretty out of it."

Not as out of it as he thought. With my heart is sinking, I take my plate and have a seat next to him. "Yeah I was."

"Figured you wouldn't remember anything the next day."

The way he says it, I wonder if that's what he wanted. To not move forward with what we started. "Anything you wanna tell me?" Here's the opening for us to discuss it all.

"Nah." He swallows, wiping his mouth. "Got you into bed with no problem. Just glad I could help."

And that's when I realize, everything I've been building up between Sully and I was completely in my head. "Yeah." I lick my lips, looking away from him, trying to hold it together. "Glad you could help too."

"HOW WAS HOUSTON?" he asks later when we sit on the couch, eating our cake, discussing the holidays.

"It was good." I let a smile work its way to my face. "I saw my parents and a couple of friends. I haven't seen them since I moved here."

"That was your first time back, right?"

"Yeah, a lot of memories." I set my cake down, pulling my knee up to my chest.

"Did something happen to make you come here? I don't think we've ever really talked about it."

I've not told anyone here about my past, but maybe it's time. "I worked for a law firm, and we were prosecuting a big drug case. One of the lead witnesses was a twelve-year-old girl who was testifying against her father. We had her in a protected location, but it wasn't enough."

"Oh, Counselor." He reaches over, grabbing my hand. His thumb strokes my palm. "Sometimes best laid plans turn into shit shows."

Don't I know it?

"Yeah, so after that happened, I couldn't stay there anymore. I didn't want to do public prosecution work anymore. That's really what we were doing, and it just didn't interest me. Not after we lost her. Life is fleeting as fuck."

"Yeah," he whispers, his eyes getting a far off look. "Yeah it is."

Maybe, just maybe the two of us have a lot more in common than we think.

CHAPTER 2
SULLIVAN

"THANK you for volunteering to work Valentine's Night," Nick says as we start the shift-change. "We would've made it work, the way we always have, but it's nicer when I can be home with the wife and kiddos, ya know?"

I don't, but I pretend like I do. "I'm sure they all appreciate it."

Nick grins. "And I appreciate when they go to bed, just leaving me and my blushing bride to do whatever we want."

Rolling my eyes, I grab a cup of the worst coffee known to man.

Welcome to Laurel Springs Police Department.

"Dude, don't remind me you're married, and have a woman to sleep next to you, and all that good stuff."

"What's up with you and Shelby?"

His southern accent makes her name almost two words. Shell Bee.

"Didn't you take her home from the Christmas Party?"

Steeling myself, I sip some of the sludge, grimacing as I

force it down. "Just because I took her home doesn't mean something happened."

He studies me a lot fucking closer than I want him to. "Yeah it did." He smirks back at me. "But I'm also getting the feeling that not a damn thing's happened since."

Glancing at my watch, I see the time. "Look, Romeo, it's clock out o'clock. Unless you wanna pull a double and take my spot. I'm sure I can go find something to do for the night."

"Fuck. That."

He rushes to clock out, before saluting me with a wave of his hand, running out the back door of the police station. I've been cornered by no more than three of my fellow officers the last week, asking me what's going on with the attorney. Interrogation avoided.

Finally some peace and quiet, allowing me to look over my duties for the night. We've called in a couple of cadets, which will let us have more cruisers on the street tonight. Even though Valentine's is supposed to be the most romantic night of the year, sometimes it can also be the deadliest.

"You riding with us tonight?"

I glance up, hearing Renegade's voice.

"Yeah, kinda surprised you're here, to be honest. Figured you'd be at home with the wife."

"She's taking Keegan for the night. Ransom and Stelle don't get too many nights off together, so when they asked, how could we say no?"

"You don't." I run a hand through my hair, taking another drink from the Styrofoam cup I hold. Hopefully this shit will perk me up and force me to stay awake. I haven't done an overnight in a while.

"Exactly. Then I'd be hearing it from both my wife and my daughter, and I make it a rule never to hear from both of them on the same subject, at the same time. Head on into the conference room so we can have our pre-shift briefing. Catch ya in a few."

THE ROOM IS quiet as we have our briefing. Renegade is the shift commander tonight, and he reminds us of some very important points. Valentine's Day can bring out the best and worst in people, just like every other fucking holiday.

I don't know what it is about the supposed happiest days of the year, maybe it's all the togetherness mixed with the alcohol? Holidays and full-moons are my least favorite shifts to work, but I do it because it's what I signed up for.

We're dismissed in a quick fifteen minutes, and everyone disperses to head out to their cars.

As we walk out, I realize I forgot a jacket, and a beanie. Northern Alabama is cold for this Southern Alabama boy, especially tonight. I can see my breath in huge puffs of white air. Here's hoping I don't have to be outside too much. If I do, I'm good and fucked.

Freezing to death isn't how I imagined I would go.

The night has been surprisingly quiet, and I'm fifteen minutes from ending my shift, when a call comes in from my apartment complex. It's a domestic, and I thank God I don't recognize the names.

"Show me as responding, dispatch," I radio in, turning on my sirens and lights.

The sun is just starting to come up over the horizon, as I head toward home. If I weren't in such a hurry, I'd stop and admire the sky. It's a fiery one this morning, full of pinks, reds, and oranges.

"I'll be responding too." I hear Tank come over the radio.

He lives the closest to me, and he's just about to go on-shift. I appreciate the fact he's willing to clock on a little early to help with what could be a potentially dangerous situation. The morning after Valentine's could be tricky.

I try to think up all the scenarios I could be walking into. That's how I was taught by my Police Chief dad. Always try to be a step ahead, be prepared for any situation you could walk into. Don't let anyone get the upper hand on you.

I've done my best to follow all of that advice since I first put on a vest and a shield. It's never steered me wrong, and I don't think it will this morning either.

Pulling up to my apartment complex, I immediately see what's happening.

"Dispatch, be advised it looks as if the female is throwing everything the male owns out of the window of their third floor apartment."

I do my best to keep the tiny grin off my face. As I see lips moving, I roll down the window so I can hear what they're saying to one another. Maybe it'll give me a clue on how to proceed.

The guy, whoever he is, is begging her to stop, promising all kinds of shit he'll probably never give her.

"C'mon, Miranda, stop it!" he yells. "You're making a scene."

"You made a scene!" she screams. "You were supposed to be working on Valentine's Day, then I walk into a restaurant with all of my friends, and there you are, having dinner with another woman. Don't tell me I'm the one making a fucking scene."

Oh shit, this is going to definitely take longer than fifteen minutes.

Tank pulls in next to me, amusement tugging at his lips too. I shake my head slightly, telling him without words now isn't the time. This girl will probably go to our homes and throw our stuff out the window too.

We both get out at the same time.

"I'll take him," he volunteers. "You're the single one, go work some of that big dick energy on her."

I roll my eyes, making a mental note to kill Ransom next time I see him. He pranked me when I joined the squad, and I still can't get people to stop talking about it. "Real funny. It's been months, when are y'all gonna let it go?"

"Never," he chuckles.

A TV crashes to the ground, causing us to turn our attention back to the arguing couple.

"Guess I better get up there," I sigh, taking the steps two at a time.

Knocking on the door with the edge of my flashlight, I announce myself. "Ma'am, Laurel Springs Police Department, please come to the door."

She shuffles around inside, and I'm met with a pair of blazing green eyes, which remind me of the one woman I can't get out of my head.

Shelby.

But now's not the time to be thinking about her. Now I need to be doing my job.

"I'm glad you're here." She opens the door wider, allowing me inside. "I want him gone from this apartment, and I never want him to be able to come back. How do I make that happen?"

Fuck my life.

"First of all, what's your name?"

"Miranda, his name is Jeff, and I want him gone."

"Well, Miranda, is his name on the lease?"

She crosses her arms, a triumphant smile on her face. "Nope."

"Does he receive his mail here? Is this his primary residence?"

The smile falters, and immediately her lower lip starts to tremble. "He does, but this is *my* apartment. I let him move in, he *promised* he was done with all the other women. I'm so damn stupid."

"No you're not, you've trusted someone who doesn't deserve it. Now we'll make this right, but if this is his residence, you'll have to speak to your landlord about evicting him."

She sniffles, nodding. "I'll see what I can do."

"And there's also that little thing of you throwing the TV down. Was that his or yours?"

"His," she mumbles. "He uses it to play his goddamn video games, when he should be spending time with me."

"We'll have to see what he wants to do about that."

"What do you mean?" She taps her foot against the floor.

"I mean you've destroyed his property."

"He destroyed my heart," she fires back, lower lip trembling again. "What can I do about that?"

"You can't send him to jail, if that's what you're wondering."

She sighs. "Alright, tell me what I've got to do to get his ass out of here. I refuse to pay his way any longer."

AN HOUR LATER, I let dispatch know I'm done for the night, and I sign off. "Thanks for coming to help me." I stop Tank, shaking his hand.

"No problem. Seems like the guy was a bit of an asshole, but other than that, it wasn't too bad."

"Oh according to her, he's the biggest asshole to ever walk this planet. I think she was hoping for an engagement ring, and he was worried about his cock ring."

Tank laughs. "No shit, he mentioned he's in school to be a fucking doctor. How many nurses will he have on a leash? He's a damn student now, not even making the bank he'll be making."

"I don't know, I almost hope your niece meets him and teaches him a thing or two."

"Stelle would eat him up and spit him out with a smile on her face."

Of that I have no doubt. "Maybe that's exactly what he needs."

We're quiet, both trying to come down from the adrenaline high you get when responding to a call.

"You should get on out of here. You're done for the night." Tank shoos me away.

"I'm pretty tired." I yawn, stretching to the sky, hoping to loosen my tight muscles. Sitting in the car for long periods of time can cause me to stiffen up. "I'll see you around."

"See ya." He waves.

Slowly, I walk back to my cruiser. Tired as hell all of a sudden. I get in and head on over to my building. All I want to do is lock up and get to my apartment. I'm contemplating on whether I should take a shower before I go to sleep or not, when I see a hot pair of legs coming down the stairs.

Immediately I know it's Shelby.

The hairs on my forearms stand at attention, and when she comes into view, I'm not disappointed. She's dressed for sin in a skirt that sits just above the knee and a fitted blazer. Her outfit screams woman of power, and I'm here for it.

Getting out of my squad car, I wave at her, watching as she walks slowly toward me.

"Heard on the scanner Miranda over in building five threw her no good, cheatin' ass boyfriend to the curb," she giggles as she looks up at me.

Most everyone looks up at me, since I'm six-three, but she doesn't have to tilt her head too far back. She's a tall woman who rocks a pair of heels.

I laugh with her. "You could say that. It was definitely one of my more interesting calls since transferring to Laurel Springs. You're getting an early start this morning."

"Yeah." She crosses her arms over her chest, rubbing her hands up and down. "I need to go to Birmingham today for a few things with my latest case. I'm hoping if I leave early enough I can miss rush hour. I have to stop by my office first though."

"It's freezing out here." I gesture to her car with a flourish.

"Not hardly," she laughs. "I went to law school in northern Kentucky. This isn't anything compared to that."

"Well you're still shivering." I point out, as we get to her car.

She hands me the keys when I hold my palm out. Getting in, I turn it on, cranking the defrost on the front and the back, as well as the heater. "Should be good to go for you in a few minutes."

"You didn't have to do that." She pushes a lock of her hair behind her ear.

"I don't mind." My gaze takes in every bit of the woman standing in front of me. "You better get going. Be safe, and if you need anything, don't hesitate to give me a call. You're one of the few who gets to break through my do not disturb."

She dips her head down, and when it comes back up, there's a smile on her face, exposing the dimple she has in her left cheek. "Thanks, Sully. I'll see you later?"

"Count on it."

Opening her back driver's side door, she puts her briefcase and bag in, before she shuts it and turns to face me. I'm almost positive it's an impulse, but I'll take it any way I can get it. She leans in, kissing me on the cheek, before pulling away and opening the driver's door.

"Sleep good."

"I will." I let her get in, then shut the door securely behind her.

Instead of walking up to my apartment, I watch as she gets situated and leaves. Feeling like a piece of myself is driving away and wondering just what the fuck I'm going to do about it.

CHAPTER 3
SHELBY

I WATCH in the rearview for as long as I can. Sullivan doesn't move, he keeps his gaze fixed on me until I round the corner, leading out to the main road.

Sullivan Baker.

I'm not sure there's ever been anyone else who's interested me as much as him. At the same time, I'm beyond positive no one has frustrated me like he has.

He thinks I don't recall the night of the Christmas party - coming so hard against his hand and on his fingers I passed out - but I do. I remember everything. I've let him believe I was too drunk to know what happened.

I wasn't.

All because I'm completely unsure of how he'll react when I tell him I know.

Late at night, I still feel him. Sometimes I use the memories to relive those moments in my head and against my hand.

The drive to my office, downtown across from Laurel Springs Police Department, takes me all of ten minutes. I snatched up this property located between the courthouse and The Café at an amazing price.

Pulling into my designated parking spot, I grab my stuff out, before I exit the car, enter my building and turn the alarm off. Even though I did my research before I came to town, and I know this is pretty much Mayberry, I still sprung for the smallest of security systems.

Laurel Springs is safe.

Safer than where I came from.

Don't think about it, Shelby. Those memories have no place in your new reality.

My old one fucking sucked, so I do my best to listen.

Once I dump everything in my office, I make a quick trip over to The Café.

Entering this place is like coming home, and a time period many have forgotten. The aroma brings back memories of my grandmother's cooking and the low-level buzz of conversation never fails to make me smile.

"Hey, girl." Violet waves over in my direction.

She seems to be helping out this morning. There's no telling who you might see in here at any given time of the day. While there are a few employees, friends and family always seem to be putting on an apron and lending a hand when it looks needed.

"Hey." I wave at her, walking up to the old-fashioned soda bar.

"Give me just a sec." She holds up her finger. "I'll be right with you as soon as I refill these coffees."

"Take your time." I have a seat, twirling around slightly on the swivel stool. This is my favorite place to sit when I come here. Giving in to the whimsy of immaturity is definitely what I need in my life.

"Morning, Shelby." I'm surprised to see Ransom behind the counter.

"Morning?"

He laughs. "I do work here from time-to-time ya know, like when my mom has a doctor's appointment, or my dad's snuck her out of town for a romantic weekend." He mimics sticking his tongue down his throat and gagging.

I laugh along with him, secretly thinking it's cute as hell his parents are still so in love, but also understanding how he might not like to be witness to it. "So which is it this time? Doctor's appointment or romantic weekend."

"Romantic weekend. Valentine's Day was yesterday, remember?"

Boy do I. Number who knows how many I've spent alone. "Which is why I'm surprised you're here."

He waggles his eyebrows, giving me a secretive smile. "Both Stelle and I were off last night. She had the early morning shift, so I volunteered. Believe me, we *celebrated* Valentine's Day."

"I keep warning him that's how he's going to have a brother or sister for Keegan." I hear Cutter as he slides in next to me. "Fucker just won't listen."

Ransom throws a few sugar packets at his brother. "You just wait, my man, when you're married and you can do whatever the fuck you want, whenever the fuck you want, you'll be the same way."

An older woman sitting beside me clears her throat.

Ransom gives her a magnificent smile. "My apologies, ma'am. What can I get you?"

"Hey, what about me?" Cutter slaps his hand on the counter, after Ransom takes her order.

"And me? I was here first," I remind him.

"The two of you wanted to give me shi- crap."

"I'm still a paying customer," I argue. "Don't make me sue you."

"Fine." He rolls his eyes, over exaggerating every move. "What do you want, Shelby?"

"Um, excuse me, where are your manners? You should take care of her first." I point to the elderly lady.

He huffs a breath, gritting his teeth if the hardening of his jaw is any indication.

When he's finally taken care of her, he comes back to me. "What can I get for you, Counselor?"

It doesn't have the same sort of impact when he says it, as it does when Sullivan let's it loose in that lazy drawl of his. In fact, I don't even like it. "A black coffee, two creams and two sugars in a to-go cup, please."

"No food?"

"Can't eat first thing in the morning, it makes me tired and throws my whole day off. I'll have some almonds and a cheese stick."

He acts like that's not enough to feed an ant, and then turns to go grab a Styrofoam cup. "Coming right up."

Cutter and I sit beside one another for a few seconds before he starts speaking. "Picked up any interesting cases lately?"

"Like I could tell you, even if I had."

"Oh c'mon, Shelby, you know I like to hear all about the weird stuff you deal with."

"So does everybody else. Doesn't mean I can talk about it."

"Oh, I know. I can still ask right?"

Ransom puts my cup down in front of me with the

requested cream and sugars. "On the house, have a good one, Shelby."

"Thanks." I leave a few dollars on the counter anyway, which Cutter grabs and puts in the tip jar. "See y'all later."

"See ya."

BUSINESS HAS BEEN SLOWER than I imagined it would since I opened up my practice almost a year and a half ago. Luckily, I had plenty of money saved up when I moved here, and my overhead costs are low.

Doesn't mean I'm not getting slightly worried though.

I've even started looking into doing other types of law. Perhaps bankruptcies and wills. It would be something to offer this small town that they don't already have.

So far there's nothing for me to sink my teeth into.

Except for one case.

Helping Karsyn Fallaway face her kidnapper at a parole hearing. Other than that, the cases have been very run-of-the-mill.

"You moved here for run-of-the-mill," I mumble.

I did, but it doesn't mean I don't want something that's going to challenge me. Something that will have me up at night reading law books. Anything that'll have me going to the state capital to check on other cases, jurisdiction, and filing motions.

There's a huge part of me that misses that aspect of my job.

But there's another part of me that remains scared of it.

The case that made me move here? I'd gotten too close, and I'd almost gotten burned.

Which is why I've traded Houston, Texas for Alabama, and why I decided to uproot my life completely. It had required a change, and by God that's what I did.

I don't regret it.

At least not all the time.

The bell over my front door rings, causing me to lift my head up in surprise. Most of the time I get phone calls or emails, not in-office visits.

When I see Violet, I give her a questioning look.

"You didn't come in for lunch, so I figured you got distracted again." She indicates the covered plate she's holding in her hand.

Looking at the clock to the left of my desk, I notice it's after two.

"I guess I did." I gratefully accept the plate she's set down and uncover it. My favorite. Meatloaf.

"If I didn't know better, I'd think you were buttering me up for something," I laugh as I dig in to the fragrant dish, accompanied with corn and green beans.

She laughs. "Not yet anyway, but who knows what the future holds. Honestly, I just worry about you." She has a seat, crossing her legs. "You remind me a lot of who I was before Anthony came into my life."

"Oh really?"

I take a drink of the water bottle I always have.

"Yeah." She tilts her head to the side. "I was running away from a lot. I had a husband who'd beat the shit out of me. There was a divorce in the process of getting finalized, but it didn't mean that he couldn't find me."

"I'm sorry." I set my fork down, taking another drink. "I've dealt with a lot of cases like that. I'm definitely not running from a husband, current or otherwise."

Her eyes are sharp, she sees a lot. "You're running from something though. So I just wanted you to know, if you ever need help, I'm here. We're here. The Laurel Springs community is pretty close-knit and you've already been welcomed in by the LSERT. If you ever need anybody to talk to, you've got it."

Suddenly my appetite isn't what it was, but I don't want to offend her by not eating more of the delicious food. I push it away slightly, running a hand through my hair. "I hear what you're saying and I appreciate it. But right now, I don't want to go into why I decided to come here."

"You don't have to." She reaches across the table, laying down a piece of paper. "This is my number. If you ever need to talk, just know I'm here."

My throat tightens and it's hard to press the words past the strangle-hold it has there.

"Thank you. I'll keep it in mind."

She nods, getting up from the seat and leaving. This time when the bell over the door rings, I'm glad to know it isn't someone coming in, but her going out.

Leaving me alone with my thoughts.

Memories, nightmares, and dreams.

Sometimes they're all the same; and I'm proof of it.

CHAPTER 4
SULLIVAN

MY FOOTSTEPS BEAT a cadence on the material of the treadmill I'm running on. A bead of sweat drips from my forehead, rolling down my nose, dangling at the very tip. Shaking my head so it'll fall off, I lift the back of my hand up to wipe at my mouth.

The heat is on in here today, because it's the end of February, and it feels every bit as such outside. But my clothing choice makes it hot too. A pair of sweatpants with a shirt and a hoodie, the hood covering my head.

Glancing down, I groan. I'm only at mile number three; I need to go five.

Especially if I want to make a spot on the Laurel Springs SWAT team.

That's been my goal since I came up here with my sister. The five-mile run is the first obstacle I have to overcome if I want to even be considered. So far, it's kicked my ass.

"Nice pace."

Ransom hops onto the treadmill beside me, warming up by walking briskly.

"Thanks, I'm trying to get it where it needs to be."

"It took me a while," he admits. "I'm not a runner, but with Rambo, I kinda have to be. It wasn't until I got partnered with him that I was even in good enough shape to try out for SWAT."

I give him a side-eye. "Can't believe you had to try out. Surprised you weren't like grandfathered in, or something."

"Nah, everybody has to get their spot the old-fashioned way here."

It makes me respect him more. "Must be nerve-wracking though."

"You ain't kiddin'. None of us who have dads that have been on the PD want to go to them and admit defeat or failure."

"That must be hard."

"And embarrassing. We're held to a higher level of standards than most other people. Which is understandable."

I may act like I don't know what he's saying, but I do. It's one of the reasons I left Paradise Lost. There, I would always be in the shadow of what my dad and brother have accomplished.

Here in Laurel Springs?

I can be me. Whoever the fuck that is.

"So," Ransom continues as he picks up the pace, starting with a slow jog. "Saw your girl the other day, she came into The Café to get her morning coffee."

"My girl?"

Everyone calls Shelby my girl, but I pretend not to be in on it.

"Yeah, you know who I'm talking about, don't even act like you don't. Everybody knows you're eyeing Shelby and she's eyeing you. When are you gonna make a move?"

"You're one to talk." I level him with a glare. "From what I heard it took Stella being in a pretty dangerous situation for you to ask her to go out with you."

"Do as I say, not as I do." He shrugs. "Besides we're married now with a super cute kid and the best dog there ever was. So…I mean I feel like I did good. I really thought after you took her home from the Christmas party, something would have happened between the two of you."

Fuck.

And I'm wearing sweatpants.

No one knows what *did* happen between us, especially Shelby. She'd passed out either before she came or after, I'm still not sure, and I haven't been able to bring myself to ask. That night had been the most exhilarating and frustrating of my life. I swear I walked around with blue balls for fucking days.

"I took her home, made sure she was good, and went to my own apartment."

It's the lie I'll tell til the day I die.

I don't want anyone to think I took advantage of her, and nor her to be embarrassed. So I live with it, trying my best every day to figure out how to bring it up.

"Sure." Ransom grins smugly. "You keep telling yourself that."

My treadmill beeps, letting me know my five miles are done. Thank God. I don't even do my cool down, I just hop off, saying some sort of goodbye to Ransom.

The last thing I need is to hear anymore love advice from him.

He's married. With a kid. Everything you thought you'd have by now, my brain mocks me.

Shut up, I scream back.

My stride is long as I head to the locker room. Normally I'd take a shower and change, but right now, I need to get out of here. For some reason it feels as if the walls are closing in, and there's nowhere for me to escape to. Going to my locker, I yank it open, grab my bag out, and make my getaway.

Once I'm in my Mustang, I hit the straight-stretch of highway next to the PD, and gun it, just to hear the roar of the engine. Something about this car always puts me in a better mood.

Hearing and feeling the power behind in palm of my hands is enough to center me and bring me down to earth.

My stomach growls causing me to look at my smartwatch. I burned over eight hundred calories, and I think I deserve some Café food.

Slowing down next to the downtown entrance, I signal a left-hand turn, looking for a parking spot. Everybody must be out and ready for lunch; everything in front of The Café is taken.

My eyes shift over to where Shelby's law office is located. Her car is there, and I wonder if she's had lunch yet.

Would I be out of line to ask her to join me? I hate eating alone, and I know she does too. Would she understand that I'm asking as more than a friend?

Probably not.

"Man the fuck up, Sullivan."

That's the problem. Last time I manned up and gave everything I had to a woman I thought I had a future with, she laughed at me.

Fucking laughed in my face.

Then turned around and got with my brother.

It hit my self-esteem hard, my self-image harder. Not the

coolest thing for a man to admit to, but it's taken me a while to recover from the blow.

Circling downtown, I finally find a spot almost as far away from The Café as I can get. Fuck it. I'll take it. Within seconds I'm parked, and out, beeping the auto locks as I pull the hood of my hoodie back over my head, doing my best to block out the cool air.

We have a new roundabout, and I swear to Jesus, only two percent of the people know how to use it. I literally wait to walk across until no one is coming, although I have the right of way. Today is not the day I wanna die.

Sprinting across the pavement, I walk up onto the curb, right in front of Shelby's office.

I'm arguing with myself, trying to figure out if I wanna bite the bullet and ask her to have lunch with me, when the decision is taken out of my hands. The door opens, and there she is.

The object of my jerk off sessions.

The star in all my erotic dreams.

Right there in the fuckin' flesh.

She turns, catching sight of me as she does. "Oh my God, hey, Sully! I was just thinking about you."

Her cheeks are bright and rosy. I'm unsure if it's from the cool weather, or her thoughts. "Oh really? What were you thinking about me for?"

"Whitney is trying to figure out a good way to raise money for the LSERT, and one of the girls suggested an auction. I thought you'd be perfect for it. You'd probably fetch the most. You're one of the city's hottest bachelors."

I don't know whether to be flattered or offended.

"Y'all were talking about auctioning me off?"

"Yeah." She grins. "Weren't you saying something the other day about needing to meet new people?"

That's not what I meant, and I'm pretty damn sure she knows it.

"Not necessarily in that way." I scratch at my chin.

"It would be for a great cause," she reminds me.

"I know, but I'll have to think about it."

Shelby's smile falters slightly and I mentally kick myself for refusing the invitation she'd eloquently extended to me. One day I'll get this shit right.

"I understand, but just so you know, you get to make all the rules of the date."

That's only appealing if I can get Shelby to participate too.

"What about women?" I ask impulsively. "Are they being auctioned off too?"

Her green eyes cloud; I can't read the emotion, but I don't back away from my question.

"Yeah, I'm one of them."

"Do you think that's wise? There's a lot of guys out there who would do something to hurt women."

She tilts her head to the side. "I lived in Houston, I think I can take care of myself, Sully."

"Be that as it may, I'd need to meet the person who gets the date with you, or you'd at least have to tell me something about it, to set my mind at ease."

This time when she looks at me, there's a sparkle in her eye. My gaze travels down to where her tongue peaks out between straight, white teeth to lick her plump, pink bottom lip.

"I was thinking something that involves chairs and handcuffs."

Suddenly I know I have to be at this auction, I have to be the one who wins the date with her. And call me crazy, but maybe she remembers a lot more from the night at the Christmas party than I gave her credit for.

CHAPTER 5
SHELBY

HE'S SPEECHLESS.

Sully keeps opening his mouth and then shutting it. No words come out, even though his throat is working so hard his Adam's apple bobs up and down. The tension between us is slightly awkward, and I do the only thing I can think of.

Invite him to lunch.

"I was about to head over to The Café. You wanna join me?"

The question seems to pull him from whatever stupor he was stuck in.

"You sure? I just worked out, and I don't smell the best. I was gonna take a shower at the station, but I had to get outta there."

"I've smelled you worse than that before," I remind him. "I am the one who helped you after the kid in the downstairs apartment puked on you."

His face flashes red before a smile tilts up the side of his full lips. "For a while I was able to forget that happened. Thanks for bringing it back up, though."

"You're welcome." I grin.

Grabbing hold of his arm, I start us walking toward the direction of what will be our lunch. My body recognizes his, and before I know it, I'm squeezing his bicep, admiring the firm muscle.

Wondering about all the other parts of him that are hard too.

When we get to the door, he opens it, holding it for me, and then a couple of older ladies. It makes my heart jump, the way he gives them a smile and acknowledges them with a nod of his head.

More than anyone I've ever met, Sullivan Baker is a good guy.

"Go ahead and sit wherever you want to, I'll be with you in a second," Leigh says as she sees us.

"Booth or table?" I look up, letting him make the decision.

He nods over to the booth across from where we stand. Sliding in, I immediately grab a menu so I don't have to meet his eyes.

Sully doesn't. He gets the same thing every time he comes here. Me? I like a little variety in my life.

I'm making a show of perusing the menu when he clears his throat. His big hands are spread across the table, and he leans in, his voice low.

"Did you mean what you said out there?"

Slowly, I put the menu down, licking my bottom lip. "Which part? I said a lot of things."

Dark eyes the color of whiskey stare back at me. An intensity I've only seen in him once before making them flare a deeper brown than normal.

"The part about chairs and cuffs." His voice is pitched so only we can hear it. "I thought you didn't remember."

For a few moments, I don't know what to say to him. It was easy to tease, especially when I wanted to shock him. But here? Right now? He's putting me on the spot. "I remember," I whisper. He probably can't even hear me.

"Why didn't you tell me?"

Apparently I was wrong, and Sully has ears like a bat. I'm saved when Leigh comes to take our orders and put the drinks she knows we always get in front of us. For as long as I can, I make a big production out of putting sugar in my tea and stirring it around, tasting it so that I'm sure it's to my satisfaction.

"I'm waiting."

He's impatient, reached the end of his rope. He wants my explanation now.

"I don't want to have this conversation here," I hiss across the table. "Not where anyone could eavesdrop."

"Then we'll take our food to go, we'll sit in my car, and you'll tell me what I want to know."

Swallowing roughly, I manage to nod. Funny how I've waited for him to ask me about this for so long, but now that I'm faced with the opportunity to lay it all out on the line - I'm shy. He gets up, signaling to Leigh.

There's no telling the excuse he's making, and when her gaze flits over to me, I want to ask. The expression on her face is one of amusement.

Nothing we did with one another was amusing.

Before I know it, he's carrying a to-go bag of food over to our booth, along with two plastic cups. Sully doesn't sit down; he takes matters into his own hands, pouring our drinks, and nodding to me. "Let's go."

This is who I'm used to, this man who takes charge and pushes ahead. It's who he was that cold night in December, and I long for more of it. We don't talk as we leave The Café. He points to his car, and together we walk swiftly. Me trying to keep up with his long legs, and him looking like he's fleeing from the devil himself.

Not even five minutes have passed when I find myself in his passenger seat, our food spread out on the console, holding my sweet tea in my hand.

His voice is hoarse, choked, almost like he's having trouble swallowing. "I'm gonna ask you again, Shelby. Why didn't you tell me you remembered?"

Grabbing a fry, I dip it in ketchup before bringing it up to my mouth.

Stalling.

I'm one hundred percent stalling.

"Stop licking the fucking ketchup off your lip and tell me."

His tone is a warning that goes straight to the spot in between my thighs.

"I didn't tell you because you never mentioned it. When you didn't mention it," - I stop for a second, running my fingers through my hair so that it covers part of my face - "I thought you regretted what happened."

"I thought *you* regretted it," he accuses.

"I didn't."

"I didn't either." His hands grip the steering wheel. "Now what do we do about it?"

That's the thousand-dollar question.

"What do you *want* to do about it?" I ask softly.

Sully runs his hands through his hair, before bringing them back down onto the steering wheel. His thumbs beat a rhythm only he can hear, but I still watch intently. Waiting to see what he does, dying to know what he's going to say.

"We're good friends." He shrugs.

My throat tightens, threatening to close, as I do my best to push the tears that are pooling in my eyes back. "We are." My voice strained to my own ears. If he can't hear it, he's fucking deaf.

"I don't have a lot of friends since I moved here," he mumbles, almost as if he's trying to convince himself we should value the friendship more than the obvious connection we have.

My stomach clenches at his words, heart threatens to beat out of my chest, and I'm doing my best not to have a full-on breakdown right here. I can feel it, the bit of hope I had for us to expand on what happened at Christmas is going down like the Titanic. I have to get out of here before I embarrass myself further. "Stop." I struggle to close the Styrofoam container. Each time I shove the tabs into the hole, it pops back out, until one of them breaks off. "Fuck!"

"Here, let me help you." He's reaching out.

"No, I got it."

"You didn't let me finish what I was going to say." His brown eyes all but pin me against the passenger door.

"I don't need to hear it. I've heard the friend-zone speech one too many times."

"It's so easy with you," he continues.

"Sullivan, I said I don't want to hear it."

When I finally get the container closed, I toss it on his dash.

"Shelby, I don't want either of us to get hurt." He grabs my hand, but I yank it away as soon as I feel the warmth of his touch.

Too late.

"I understand." I chew on my bottom lip to keep from sobbing. "But right now I have to go to an appointment I forgot about."

"Shelby, you don't understand." He tries to soften the blow, but it's there. A huge hole in my stomach - big as a cannon blast.

"Sorry, I should have remembered. My client will probably be pissed."

"Shelby, stop."

Opening the door, I step out with one leg, before turning to face him. "I'll see you around the apartment complex?"

Before he can say anything else, I'm out the door, speed walking to my office, praying to God he doesn't follow me. I need to fall apart, then put myself back together, and I need to do it in private.

How stupid could I have been to think he'd want more from me than one night of a good time?

He didn't even get the good time. Reaching down, I take off my heels, and finish the sprint to my office.

Opening the door, I throw the shoes on the ground, and then hurriedly lock it, collapsing against the solid wood. It's strong enough to take the weight of me and ten others, but I'm not sure it can withstand the heaviness of my broken heart.

I let the tears fall, stream down like rain. My breath comes in huge gulps as I struggle across the hall to where the bathroom is.

"It's okay," I whisper. "You'll be fine, Shelby. You'll pull through this and come out on the other side like you always do."

Taking a few deep breaths, I do my best to calm down.

Eventually the tears stop and I get some paper towels to wipe off my face. Looking in the mirror is jarring. My makeup is wrecked; mascara and eyeliner are smudged and all the lipstick is chewed off my lips.

"This isn't the end of the world," I say out loud as I start to repair the smudged makeup. "You never really had him, girl."

But I'm seriously not sure if I'll be able to repair the damage to my heart as easily.

CHAPTER 6
SULLIVAN

I WATCH HER RUN AWAY, glued to my seat.

Get up!

Go after her!

But I can't seem to make myself move. This didn't go the way I imagined it would at all. In my mind I'd always pictured us talking about the night of the Christmas party in a controlled environment. We would laugh remembering how hot we were for one another, then we'd admit we both had feelings for each other, ending with a fucking replay of what happened that night.

The only thing I can do is beat my palm against the steering wheel. Why didn't I go after her?

Inhaling deeply, I grab up the food and take it over to one of the homeless men who uses our square as his home. I've completely lost my appetite. Irritated beyond belief, I start up the car and head toward the apartment complex I call home.

Halfway there, my phone rings. For two seconds I think

about not picking it up, but when I see the smiling face of my sister, I answer quickly.

"Hey."

"You sound extremely excited to hear from me. Are you okay, Sully?"

What I wouldn't give to lay all this down at her feet, but she's probably calling me about wedding preparations and there's no way I'm going to take away the joy of this time in her life. "I'm fine, just had a rough day. What's happening?"

"Cutter told me he hasn't been able to touch base with you yet, but he wants you to be one of his groomsmen."

The heaviness of my heart lifts slightly. No matter how I'm feeling about my own life, Ro and Cutter have one of the best things going I've ever seen. "He wants me to be a groomsman?"

"Yeah, I know it doesn't mean as much coming from me, but we're trying to tag-team this wedding."

"No, I understand we've been busy as hell too. Neither one of you owe me an explanation. What do I need to do?"

"Get fitted for your tux within the next week? We don't have a whole lotta time."

The way she's speaking makes the hair on the back of my neck stand on end. "I thought you two weren't in a big hurry. Why within the next week?"

She's quiet in a way that makes me nervous. I've heard my sister quiet before, and this kind of silence almost has me turning the car around and heading to the ambulance bay to beat Cutter's ass.

"Nothing bad." I can hear the smile in her voice. "I found out yesterday I'm pregnant," she whisper-shouts to me. "You're the first person I've told, and I wish I could do it in person, but you know how life is right now. We want to get married before I start showing."

I have to pull over to the side of the road. "Ro? You're pregnant?"

"Barely," she whispers. "We haven't been trying, but we haven't been preventing either. Both of us knew we wanted kids, so we went for it. It happened a lot sooner than we expected."

"Are you okay with it?"

Knowing how she lost Etta, I want to make sure her mental health is taken care of.

"I am, I'm excited. We plan on getting married in the next two to three months. Ruby and Whitney are working on it together," she mentions members of the Kepler family who run an event planning business. "They assured me they'd be able to make this happen. Hell, Whitney even came out of retirement for it."

"This is what you want?"

"This is exactly what I want, Sully. It's everything with the right man."

"I'm happy for you, Ro, so happy."

"Thanks, Sully, I'm happy too."

We hang up, and immediately I have a feeling of loss. Of never having what she has. Letting moments slip through my fingers and not forcing myself to make others understand. The look in Shelby's eyes as she walked away from me, it's haunting.

Raindrops splash against the windshield, fat drops, making noise. It reverberates in the quiet of my car, hitting the roof, the asphalt I'm driving on. Most of all, the sound knocks against a place inside my head. A place that's stubbornly shoved people away from me for so long. When Etta died, it affected us all.

Ro lost trust.

I lost the ability to freely give my emotions to anyone who didn't know me before.

Before our hearts were broken by a little girl with a smile as bright as the sun. Before I had to be a pallbearer to a teeny, tiny casket, light enough I could have carried it on my own. Would have if anyone had asked. She was a light in the darkness, and when her flame was snuffed out, my family lost a piece of themselves. Me? I lost a piece of my heart. One I haven't been able to recover, let alone give to anyone else.

But those eyes of Shelby's?

They remind me of Etta's. The way she trusted me?

I saw that in Shelby the night of the Christmas party. "What do I do, Etta?"

I whisper the question, not knowing if it's a question I should be asking of a little girl who never even had her fifth birthday.

All of a sudden, a deer appears in the middle of the road, causing me to slam on my brakes. Oil on the asphalt spins me around once, twice, maybe even three or four times. When I slide to a stop, my car is facing back the way I was coming. The front-end headed toward town instead of my apartment.

Smirking, I can't help the chuckle pulled from my throat. "I got it, E. I got it."

The whole way back to Shelby's office my mind is racing as fast as the miles my car eats up. I hope like hell she hasn't left, that I haven't managed to fuck up the chance I had with her. This woman, she admitted she remembered what happened, and I didn't give her the answers she wanted.

That's my fault, and I hope she's way more forgiving than I typically am.

Pulling along the square, I see her car is still sitting in front of her office building. I come to screeching halt next to it, throw it in park, before opening the door and running into the deluge of water pouring down. Approaching her office, I can see the entrance she normally has open is shut, and when I try the knob it's locked.

"Shelby!"

My fists beat against the wood, hoping she can hear me.

"Shelby!"

Right now I wish I had my toolkit; I could pop this lock in a few seconds.

"Shelby!"

I scream again, hoping she'll hear the desperation in my voice.

"What?"

I have to stop my fist from hitting her in the face when she swings the door open, standing there with her arms crossed over her chest.

She's never looked hotter than she does right now. All full of irritation and anger.

"I'm sorry," I start.

"You should be." She taps her foot on the floor. "Do you know what it took for me to tell you I remembered the night of the Christmas Party, Sullivan? Nobody has ever done what you did to me that night, I've never responded to another person the way I did with you."

I hold my hand up, cutting her off. "Look, Counselor, you got to talk in the car, now I get to talk."

She looks like she wants to argue, but I muscle my way in, shutting the door with my foot, locking it so we don't get disturbed and closing anyone else out of this very private conversation we're about to have.

"I'm waiting." She tilts her chin.

"Fuck, you're hot." I close the distance between us, shoving my hands into her hair, tilting her head to my liking. "You don't know how many times I've jacked off to the night of the Christmas Party, how many times I wanted to ask you about it. You never gave me any inkling you remembered it, so I didn't. Today you took me by surprise and I didn't know how to react."

"But you do now?" She baits me.

"I do." I swallow deeply, pulling one hand back to rub my thumb over her full bottom lip.

"How are you going to react?"

Her pulse is thumping at her throat, her tits are pressing against my chest with her shallow breathing, emerald eyes are dilated as they gaze into mine.

"How I should have reacted thirty minutes ago," I whisper before I take her mouth.

It's an aggression, a show of ownership I've never given another woman, but there's something about Shelby Bruce that gets to me. She's under my skin, a scent in my nose, a taste in my mouth. My lips eat hers up as she gives into the kiss I've wanted to take for months.

Her fingers gouge at my back, fisting at the hoodie covering my body. Mine destroy her hair, moving down her torso to her ass. The skirt she wears prevents me from doing much, but I manage to pull it up slightly. Enough so that I can get access to her thighs and ass. Palming the globes, I lift her up, pulling her legs around my waist as I walk her over to the couch along the wall.

Having a seat, I lean back so she can straddle me and

rock her hips against my hard cock. When we pull apart, it's because we can't breathe. As we suck in air, I manage to speak.

"Is this okay with you?"

"Hmm, totally okay," she moans as I move my hand up, curling around her left breast, worrying the peaked nipple with my thumb.

"Good." I pull her back to me, kissing her with everything I've got.

She's fighting against my damp hoodie, trying to get it off my body when we both hear a loud knocking at the door.

"Shelby, it's time for my appointment. Are you here?"

"Shit," she whispers, dropping her forehead against mine. "I really do have a client."

"Fuck," I groan along with her. "The sounds like Widow Haley."

"It is." She gets off me, trying to straighten herself out. "I'll be with you in just a moment, Mrs. Haley."

"What the fuck am I supposed to do with this?" I point to my sweatpants, where anyone who looks at me can see how ready I was to get busy with Shelby here in her law office.

"Think about people in their underwear," she giggles.

"Doesn't work, I'm just gonna think about you."

She gives me a look, wiping off her lips, with an indulgent grin on her face. "I need you to get out of here so I can do my job. There's a bathroom over there." She points to the right to a room I haven't seen before. "If you want to take care of business so you can leave."

"Shelby!"

"Coming, Mrs. Haley. I've really got to go." She looks up at me.

"Stop by my apartment when you get off work." I grab her hand, kissing the palm. "We need to talk."

"We do." She points at me. "And I mean *talk*."

I wink. "We'll talk."

"I mean it, Sully."

"I do too, Counselor. I do too."

CHAPTER 7
SULLLIVAN

DRIVING HOME IS uncomfortable in many ways. The biggest one is between my thighs. Going to the bathroom at Shelby's office did absolutely nothing for the hard-on I'm still sporting. Feeling the material of my sweatpants against the sensitive head of my dick isn't making the situation any better.

Parking, getting out, and taking the stairs two at a time doesn't do anything either. Even slamming my front door fails to give me satisfaction. Neither does throwing off my clothes as I walk through my apartment toward the bathroom, letting them land where they may.

Cranking the hot water, I let it run for a few minutes as I try to talk myself out of what I'm about to do.

It would be wrong.

But it would feel so good.

It wouldn't be any different than what you've been doing since you moved here.

My thoughts are getting on my damn nerves.

Pushing the curtain back, I get in, though the flow is still cold. I'm annoyed as it does nothing to relieve the throbbing between my legs.

The entire time I'm in here, I argue with myself. To take pleasure, or live with the irritation. For longer than I care to admit, I've done the second. Mostly because I felt like our whole family was being punished for losing Etta. Now that Rowan has found her happiness, the dark cloud that's seemed to encompass us is lifting.

The sun is brighter, the sky is bluer, and I'm not frowning all the time. But that still doesn't make it okay for me to jack off to my neighbor. Does it?

Turning the water off, I press my forehead against the tiles, rolling it around for a few seconds, hoping for my thoughts to clear. When they don't, and my cock jumps at the memory of the kiss we shared, I stomp out of the shower, through the doorway, and down the hall. When I get to my bedroom, I push the covers off, lay on my back, and situate myself against the mattress.

Tilting my head into the pillow, I close my eyes, thinking about the woman whose got my emotions spinning out of control. Shelby isn't at all what I expected when I came to Laurel Springs, but fuck if she's not exactly what I've needed.

A hazy fantasy begins to concoct itself in my head. One where we didn't have to stop in her office. Where I cleaned off the desktop with one sweep of my arm before bending her over at the waist.

Tits down, ass up.

My breathing becomes labored as I go deeper into the fantasy, imagining reaching down, grabbing her skirt and wrenching it up over her cheeks.

There it is. The string of a thong nestled for me to latch onto. Using my fingers, I pull the fabric out, wrapping it around my wrist.

"Sully," she gasps.

"Do you want me to stop?"

Shelby looks over her shoulder at me. Those green eyes of hers hooded with passion. "No." She shakes her head. "Please don't stop."

With my other hand, I tuck my thumb into my palm and extend my middle and index finger as I lift up to her mouth. "Open for me, Counselor."

She accepts my fingers, twirling around them with her tongue, bathing the flesh with moisture that'll ease my way into her body. When I go to extract them, she sucks, refusing to release. "You want something else to suck on?" *I breathe into her ear.* "I've got six and a half inches, right here."

A groan rips from her throat as I move my wet fingers between her thighs, holding them open with my own. I take her in increments. "You're tight." *My words are a hiss as I do my best to be patient.*

"It's been a while, Sullivan. More than likely longer for me than it has for you."

"I wouldn't count on that, darlin'."

Her head tilts forward as she accepts my invasion, rocking back against my fingers. "Oh my God."

"Yeah?" *I crowd into her, getting all up in her personal space.* "You like that?"

She nods. "Mmm hmm."

Using my fingers I widen her passage, getting her ready for my length. With my other hand I lift her upper body off the desk. Sliding my palm up to her throat, I circle my fingers around the flesh, feeling it move as she swallows roughly.

Pulling her neck back, I make a spot big enough for me to move in, open-mouth going after her skin. She squirms as I suck, lick, bite, kiss, and blow against the hot surface, wiggling at my fingers still inside her.

"Sullivan!" she screams, panting, her hands reaching back to grip my thighs tightly. Holding me as close as I can get, until she's coming against my hand, riding it with her head tilted on my shoulder. Inhaling huge gulps of air.

Instead of letting her ease herself down, I quickly push my sweatpants and underwear below my dick, grasp my length in my hand for a few seconds and give it a quick jerk before I place it at the opening of her pussy, and slide fucking home.

This is when it stops being a fantasy and I realize I'm grasping myself in my palm, jacking the tight skin of my hard cock furiously. My thighs press up into my strokes, my other hand moves down my legs to scoot past my length and grab my balls. They're tight, drawn up between my thighs, kissing the skin as they wait to be emptied.

"Fuck," I moan, my head thrashing on the pillow as I go between the fantasy and the reality, wishing like hell I was pressing into Shelby's body instead of my own hand.

"Goddammit," launches out of my mouth in a snarled whisper.

Fuckin' hard as a rock and can't seem to make myself come. Desperation grabs at my stomach, causing my abs to tighten.

My whole fucking body is on a string as I continue to move my hand at a furious pace. Up my length and then down, collecting the fluid at the tip to ease my way.

"Come on." I strain, wanting so badly to push past whatever barrier is keeping me from spilling against my stomach.

After a few minutes of being so close I can taste it, I drop my cock, twitching as it brushes my belly button, leaving a trail of fluid behind. "Son of a bitch," I groan as I roll over onto my side, yanking a box out from underneath the bed.

It isn't often I have to use this toy box, but sometimes it's a must. Especially when I've been on edge for far too long. Popping the top off, I reach in, grabbing a bottle of lube and a damn pocket pussy. I would be disgusted in myself if it wasn't for how horny Shelby's got me.

"Fuck yes," I moan as I sink my length into the toy, closing my eyes at the feel of it. It's not the same as a real, live person, but it's enough for times like this.

Pushing up onto my knees, I fuck down into it, while running my other hand over my stomach. My skin is sensitive to the touch, having been on edge for far too long. All I can do is grunt and feel, imagine I'm plunging deep into her body, pretend like it's her walls squeezing me tightly. Taking a break, I turn around so that I can grab hold of the headboard.

Gripping the wooden edge hard enough I could snap it in two, I use it to leverage myself. It allows me to thrust deeper and faster, my balls slapping against my thighs as I continue. My body is curled up tighter than it's ever been.

Closing my eyes I tilt my head back, gritting my teeth, grasping the headboard, and fucking my hand with everything I have.

Finally.

"Oh my God, fuck yes," I grunt and groan as my orgasm overpowers me. "Shelby," I whisper when her green eyes appear in my mind. "Goddamn." I continue thrusting through it, panting as I lose my balance and fall on my back.

Chest heaving, hair sticking to my forehead, and a depleted cock in my hand, I lick my lips and sigh. If I ever get inside her, once won't be enough.

I have a strange premonition I'll never be able to stop, and surprisingly that's okay with me.

CHAPTER 8
SHELBY

MY MIND ISN'T where it should be - on Mrs. Haley's will. Instead, I'm thinking about the man who left my office as she came in. Sullivan's been occupying more of my attention than he should, but what a welcome distraction that man is.

As I look over the papers she's brought, I softly sigh. This is the type of shit I hate doing, but it pays the bills. Thinking of a person no longer living has always been a trigger for me. I don't like considering end-of-life measures or procedures, but it's part of the job. A well-paying one, at that.

Especially when I don't have people knocking down my door to be represented.

Don't think about it, Shelby. You've never been in it for the money.

But, my mind argues, it's something we need to have in order to live and eat.

"I don't want my grandson to get anything, Shelby." She slaps her frail hand down on my desk.

"I'll make sure of it," I assure her for the hundredth time.

Her hand; the sight of it causes my stomach to clench.

What I know were once strong are now bony, with paper thin skin stretched over top. Little brown blemishes dot here and there. A wedding ring, looking as if it's been molded to her, still sits on her left hand.

"Mrs. Haley. How long has your husband been deceased?"

I can't stop myself from asking the question. Maybe it's because I've never had anyone who wanted to marry me, but my brain won't quit focusing on it.

"Goin' on twenty years now." She smiles sadly. "Didn't think I'd make it this long without him, but I've surprised everyone, including myself."

"Why are you here?" Another one that I can't keep from asking. "He's been gone so long, why are you rewriting the will?"

I've wondered this since the first time she came into my office. The original will she placed on my desk had been drafted almost forty years before. It was weathered; the pages were yellowed on the edges and smelled of cigarette smoke. She's never been honest with me when I ask, but I continue to. Someday she'll have to tell someone.

She shifts in the seat, crossing one thin leg over the other, leaning toward my desk. The way she slumps emphasizes the slight hunch in her back. "My grandson," she starts.

It's on the top of my tongue to ask about her children, but I stop myself, letting her tell the story in her own way.

"He's my next of kin. I've outlived my husband and my daughter."

"I'm sorry to hear that, Mrs. Haley."

Her brown eyes get a faraway look and the sides crinkle. I wonder what she's remembering as she smiles.

"My daughter, Isabelle, passed away ten years ago this

winter. The breast cancer got her, and now it's gotten me," she whispers, eyes moving down toward the floor.

God, this gets worse the more I hear.

"I always thought I had time," she continues. "Would be able to get my grandson to make changes in his life, but my time is running out."

"What do you mean?" I need to have a full view of the picture before I can help.

"The doctors have said the cancer has spread. There's nothing else they can do. Soon, they'll be calling in hospice care and I'll see my husband and daughter again. I can feel it." She rubs her arms. "The chill as I near the end of my life. Knowing I won't be here for the holidays, or to see another birthday, but I'm resigned and ready."

"What is it you exactly want to do?"

"I want to make sure Frank Gentry doesn't get anything of mine. Whether it be money, property, or the toilet paper I wiped my ass with."

It's tough, but I manage to hide the laugh that threatens to escape. She may be eighty-six-years-old, but she's spry, and obviously has hard feelings toward her grandson. "Is there anything I should know about?" I pull my legal pad closer to my body, pen poised to take notes. "If he might hurt you, I need to know about it."

She gets that far-off look in her eyes again. "It's not me he might hurt." The sigh that escapes her chest rattles with the sound of a thousand secrets she must be keeping. "It's his wife," she whispers. "I want to leave everything to her, but only if she divorces him."

My head snaps back on my neck. These were the last words I expected to hear from her. "I'm sorry? You want her to divorce him?"

"Yes, she's a sweet girl and she doesn't deserve what he does to her."

My mouth gets dry, throat tightens. "What does he do to her, Mrs. Haley?"

She licks her lips, like she has the same reaction as I did. Getting up, I get us both some water, before I sit back down.

"It's imperative I know. That way I can be prepared if he chooses to fight."

"Can he do that? I thought making the will would prevent him from doing so."

"He can try, but I won't let him win," I assure her. "Having said that, I need to know what he does to his wife. What does he do to you?"

Mrs. Haley's hand shakes as she sets down the glass of water. I'm unsure if it's from old age, or fear. Either of them piss me off. She finally speaks.

"He doesn't do anything to me. I haven't let him in years. It's his wife. The things he does to her..." She shakes her head.

"Please tell me."

"He beats her," she whispers. "He beats her badly. For some reason Montana won't leave. She loves him."

Furiously, I scribble on my legal pad. "It happens to a lot of women. Their abusers isolate them, and they start to believe the only person they can count on is the abuser."

She nods. "That's exactly what he's done to her."

It makes me sick to my stomach when I hear about things like this. "Okay." I jot down a few notes, trying to think on the go. "We need to prepare in case he does fight her getting your estate. Have the police ever been called on him?"

"Yes, like clockwork every two weeks. That's the longest he can seem to go without punishing her."

"What's he punishing her for?"

"I don't know." She rubs at her face. "I've tried to ask and he acted like he wanted to get violent with me." Her voice shakes. "If he were to hit me the way he hits her, he'd kill me with the first punch, so I stopped asking."

"Every two weeks?"

"Every two weeks."

"I've got some good information here. Let's meet again on Tuesday. Is that good for you? I'll have a draft of the will and hopefully I'll have some information on Frank. Is Frank his real name?"

Her eyes lower, like she's ashamed for telling me about him.

"It's normal, Mrs. Haley. It's normal to feel as if you're tattling on a loved one. Part of the abuse. Trust me when I say you aren't the first, and you won't be the last. Perhaps, though, you can save Montana's life. I'd have to think no one else has thought about her in that way for a while."

"Her family doesn't speak to her anymore. He's pushed them so far out of her life, I'm not sure they'll ever be able to heal the wound."

"Hopefully they'll be able to. It takes a little bit, but once she's away from him, she'll heal."

"Who's to say this will convince her to leave?"

Flipping over the paperwork she's given me, I check the dollar amount Mrs. Haley's putting in her trust. "I'd say two point five million would be enough for anyone to leave. She can do a lot with money like this."

"So could he, if he were able to get it."

"Which is why I need you to tell me if Frank is his given name," I guide her delicately back to the question I asked before.

"It's Franklin," she answers. "Franklin Beaumont Gentry."

"That's a damn mouth full," I mumble.

She laughs slightly. "Big name was meant to be for a big man. We had huge dreams for him; all of us did. He was going to sit in the Senate. Make Laurel Springs and this family proud."

I don't want to ask, but at this point nothing can stop me. I have to know the whole story. "What was his failure to launch?"

"Being spoiled was the first problem. That was partially thanks to us, and then his mother who wanted to make up for an absentee father. But what really did it was when he found the drugs."

"He's a drug addict?" I make another note.

"Supposedly recovering." She rolls her eyes. "I'll believe it when I see it. He's been to numerous rehab programs in the last fifteen years. Nothing's ever stuck."

"This gives me a lot to go on. I'll be doing some background work. Is there anything you want to warn me about? Anything you don't want me to look into? If there are skeletons in the closet, now's the time to tell me, Mrs. Haley."

"None in mine, dear." She reaches over the desk, patting me on the hand. "Mine came out in the open years ago. I have nothing to hide."

I turn my hand over, grasping hers. "I'll make sure this goes the way you want it to."

"I know you will, Shelby. I'm counting on you."

"And I promise not to let you down."

She gets up to leave, and I walk her out, before grabbing my briefcase and purse, heading straight for Laurel Springs PD.

CHAPTER 9
SHELBY

"YOU'RE NOT TELLING me what I wanna know, Ransom." I blow out a breath, annoyed at the man standing in front of me.

He adjusts his stance, crossing his arms over his chest. Rambo whines, sitting at attention. The dog knows me, I reach out and give him a pet on the head. When I look back up at Ransom, he's side-eyeing me.

"Shelby, if it were up to me, I'd give you the info you want, but you have to make an open records request. It's an ongoing investigation."

"That's horseshit and you know it. If I'd been listening to the scanner, I would've heard it."

"Then I suggest you get a scanner, or talk to your BFF Sullivan and see if he can help you."

This time I cross my arms over my chest, tilting my head to the side. "I have a scanner. Don't be a dick, Ransom."

He chuckles, uncrossing his arms and running a hand down his face. "Not my intention, Counselor."

"Don't call me that," I snap.

"But it's okay for Sully to call you that, huh? I'm tellin' ya. Go talk to him, he'd probably get you what you want to know."

"Don't do me any favors, Thompson."

A smirk works across his face. It gives the impression he was a super cutie kid before he turned into the man he is now, and even that pisses me off. "Wouldn't dream of it, Counselor."

"Oh, screw you."

I turn to walk out of Laurel Springs PD, but a whine stops me in my tracks. Pivoting on my heels, I go back to where Rambo stands, reach down and give him a few more head scratches, before he puts his paw up for me to shake. Obliging him, I coo, "You're such a good boy. I have no idea how you turned out so sweet when your owner's such a douche canoe."

"Douche canoe?" He snorts, laughing loudly.

Ignoring him, I walk out of the building and to my car. When I get in, I'm still fuming, but I'm beginning to think he's right. The person who can help me is the one that's waiting on me to get home.

FORTY-FIVE MINUTES later I knock on Sully's door, holding a bottle of Southern Comfort in one hand and a jug of Milo's Sweet Tea in my other. He leans in the doorway, looking like a fucking model, wearing a grin on his face.

"What?" I ask when I can no longer stand it.

"Got a few texts from Ransom."

I roll my eyes, waiting for him to let me in. "Did he tattle on me?"

His gaze drops down to where I hold my drinks. "You hoping to get me feelin' good and then question me about the info you need for your client?"

Now that pisses me off. Stepping up to him, I stand on my tiptoes. Gone are my professional clothes, and along with those are the heels that put me in the vicinity of his height. Now I wear a pair of cut-off shorts, flip-flops, and a t-shirt. Even though it's chilly, I know things between us are bound to heat up. "No, I was hoping to have an adult conversation and some adult beverages with you. The only way I wanted to get you feeling good was with my mouth on yours."

Those brown eyes of his get darker, his eyelids come down slightly. "Yeah?" he asks before he bites his lip, tilting his head closer to mine.

"Yeah. The only way this is gonna work is if we're honest with each other, Sullivan."

"Agreed. So, Shelby what are we? Friends with benefits? Trying to have a relationship?"

I've thought about this more than I care to admit. "How about we see where it goes? Expectations lead to disappointment, and I never want that with you."

Making a noise in the back of his throat that appears to be agreement, he reaches out with his big hand to cup my hip.

Fucking finally.

Feels like thirteen thousand years I've been waiting for him to touch me.

"Whatever happens with the job won't affect us," I whisper.

"Promise?" His skin his hot as it touches me between the waistband of my shorts and the hem of my shirt.

"Promise."

He's leaning in farther, and I open my mouth in anticipation of this kiss I've wanted all afternoon.

"We can still discuss things, right?" he rushes in a jumble of words.

"Yes," I snicker. "We can still discuss things, but neither one of us is going to use the other to get what we need."

"Oh, there's a lot I need you can help me with, Counselor."

And with those words he closes the distance between us. His kissable lips meet mine, and I almost drop the bottle of Southern Comfort as I go to wrap my arm around him. He hooks his finger in my belt loop, pulling me toward his body. If I knew it wouldn't make a mess, I'd let everything go and wrap my legs around his waist right now.

When he pulls back, I stumble and without his strong presence I might have fallen at his feet. "You better go ahead and come on inside." He moves to let me in.

It's hard to walk with my knees weak, but I do. Going over to his counter, I put our drinks down before turning to rummage in his cabinets for two glasses. I've been here enough times that I know exactly where to go, but I'm looking for one in particular. A plastic tumbler with a Texas Longhorn logo on it.

He eyes the cup in my hand. "I can't believe you put that piece of shit in my cabinet."

I grin, putting the plastic cup under his ice dispenser in the door. When I have enough, I start mixing my SoCo and iced tea. "Call it a piece of shit all you want, Sully. At any time you coulda thrown it away, but yet here it is. Each and every time I come here and go to make myself a drink. It's in the back, but it's always there."

"Hmm."

"Stop grunting like a cave man. Do you want one?" I tip my drink to him.

"Not in that cup, I don't."

"What?" I put the lip up to my mouth, licking the residue off of it.

His body tightens, his eyes flash with something I've never seen before.

"You don't wanna put your mouth where mine's been?"

I don't know who this woman is that all of a sudden became outspoken and such a tease, but I'm not ready to put her back under wraps yet.

"I'll put mine where yours has been all day, but not on a Longhorn cup. I'll get what I need right from the source."

He watches as I take a drink and set the cup down. Before I know it, he's around the counter, his hands in my hair, tilting my head back, and claiming my mouth with his. For long seconds his tongue pushes against mine, tangling this way and that. When he pulls away, I'm unsure what time it is and how long we've been standing in his kitchen.

"You wanna make me one of those?"

The tone of his voice sends chills up and down my arms. Aroused, southern, a tinge of longing. It's all there and at the same time, it's all mine.

"Sure you don't wanna drink mine?" I smirk.

"We talked about that."

"We did, didn't we?"

I pull away, going about making him the drink he requested. Sullivan has a seat at the bar, watching as I work. "So what did you go talk to Ransom about?"

Turning to look at him over my shoulder, I put a hand on my hip as I get his ice. "Like he didn't tell you? That man has a mouth a mile wide."

He laughs. "Ransom can keep a secret when he needs to."

"I'll believe it when I see it."

"That's the thing." Sullivan pushes his hair out of his eyes. "You'll never see it, 'cause he'll never reveal it."

"Whatever you say. I'm sure he told you what I was there for."

When I hand him his drink, he takes a big one, before he sets the glass down, eyes locked on mine. "Frank Gentry isn't someone to mess with, Shelby."

Ransom did tell him what I wanted.

"I'm not messing with him; I'm simply trying to find out information."

"Being curious about someone like him isn't smart."

My mood deflates slightly. "You won't help me?"

"It's not that I don't want to, but like Ransom said, it's an ongoing investigation. You'd have to file an open records request and we both know how long that could take."

"Why is it an investigation?"

"I wish I could tell you, Counselor, but I can't."

Frustrated, I take another drink. "Are you telling me what Ransom did?"

"What did he tell you?"

"To get a damn scanner and listen. Since I already have one at home, I'm considering getting one for my office."

Throwing his head back he laughs so hard I have to join in. "Sometimes Ransom is too smart for his own good."

"A smart*ass*," I correct him, brushing tears of laughter from my eyes.

"Yeah, heard you called him a douche canoe, gave Rambo some love, and then walked out."

"See? He's a gossip."

"Didn't say I heard all that from Ransom."

"Then who'd you hear it from?"

His lips spread into a huge smile. "Wouldn't you like to know?"

"Are you gonna tell me?"

"Depends." He reaches over, grabbing a lock of my hair with his fingers. Slowly, he twirls it around the knuckle, before letting it go.

"Depends on what?"

"On if you've been good enough to deserve the answer or not."

"I assure you, Sully. I'm always good."

"Same goes, Shelby. Same goes."

CHAPTER 10
SULLIVAN

"IF MY MAMA FOUND OUT, she'd kill me." I wave off the money Shelby is trying to force into my hand. "Besides, you brought the drinks." I pick my cup up, downing it as I make my way to the door. The doorbell rings again. "Coming."

"That'll be twenty-three even."

I put thirty in the delivery guy's hand. "Keep the change."

Shelby's at my kitchen counter again, mixing herself another drink. "You sure you want a second one so quick?"

"Today's been a real shit day, Sully." She uses her finger to stir, before bringing it up to her mouth.

The way she closes her lips around the tip goes right to my dick. I know she didn't mean for it to, but I'm a man who finds her attractive. I can't seem to help it. Walking over, I grab her hand, before bringing it up to my lips. "Why don't you let me make it better for you?"

Her eyes are dark as she watches my movements, seeming to take in every single one.

"Oh yeah?" She brings her bottom lip in between her teeth. "What would you do to make it better for me?"

There's only one thing I can say. "Whatever you want me to."

Lifting her cup off the counter, she takes a long swallow. "You know what I want more than anything?"

"What?"

Shelby comes closer, sidling up to my body. Her fingers grip my t-shirt. The low-level buzz that's always between us amps up in volume. The words she speaks are barely above a whisper, but they could be a shout in this room because it's so quiet. "I want you to give me what it is you think I want. I make decisions all the time." She curls her finger under the hem of my shirt. "When I'm with you, I don't want to think. I just want to feel."

Reaching out, I tip her chin up with my finger. "Are you sure, Shelby? I might be more than you bargained for."

"And I might be able to take way more than you ever imagined."

With her other hand, she has another drink, but as she brings the cup down, I remove it from her grasp, tipping it back into my mouth, getting rid of the remaining liquid. A noise of irritation slips across her lips, causing them to open slightly.

It's all I need to take what I want.

Her mouth.

I've never found one that fit mine quite like hers does. It should scare me to death, but this is Shelby – and if there's anything I know about her – she won't stand for me running scared. She'll drag me back to her handcuffed and hogtied.

To be honest, that's kinda what I like about her.

Fusing my lips to hers, I bend at the knees, cupping her

ass in my hands, and lift her on top of the counter. Once there, she spreads her legs wide for me, giving enough room for me to be all up in her business.

Our tongues tangle, much like they did this afternoon, but now there's an urgency we didn't have before. One born of being interrupted and not getting to finish what we started.

Moving my hands from her ass, I play with the hem of her shirt, slightly asking for permission by barely running my finger along the smooth skin of her stomach. The moan against my mouth is all I need to slip underneath the fabric and push it up her body.

We separate so I can lift it off.

Just barely.

Only long enough to take a breath.

Then we're back together, fused like superglue. Her fingers grip the belt-loops of the old, comfortable jeans I wear, pulling me tighter into her. So tight, I have to break our connection.

"Sully," she whisper-pants. "I ache for you."

I've wanted to hear those words since the night of the Christmas party. Lord knows I've ached for her too.

"Where?" My voice is deep, full of desire with a side of teasing as I move one hand to her neck, the other to her lace-encompassed tit. Gently, I press into her throat, before palming the breast. "Right here?"

"Yes." She throws her head back, pushing her tits closer to my gaze. Slightly I raise my hand to the edge of the lace. If there's one thing I know about Shelby now, it's that she has excellent taste in panties and bras. Pulling it down, I expose the upper swell, and then the nipple. It juts out, begging for my touch. I do one better; I lean in, closing my lips around it.

"Sully." The guttural groan hits me right in my dick, causing it to punch harder against my jeans.

With my hand still around her neck, I press her back flush with the countertop, slowly lowering her until she's lying flat. Her hands move to my head, tangling in the hair that's gotten too long.

"I need to cut it," I mumble, my lips leaving a trail of moisture on her skin.

"Don't." She yanks hard. "I like it."

Lifting my head up, I smirk. "Your wish is my command, Counselor."

"Then I wish you'd take these clothes off and put your mouth everywhere." She smirks back at me.

Not one to let a challenge go unanswered, I make quick work of her cutoffs and panties, then pull the cups of her bra down her chest. Our eyes meet for a millisecond. "You might wanna hold on." The words are said on a sigh.

"To what?" She looks around.

I spread out, taking her hands and entwining her fingers with mine, pressing them to the cool surface of the counter. "To me."

That's when I hit my knees. Being tall and living in an apartment has its advantages. My shoulders make all the room I need before I clasp my mouth against her core, going at her hard from the moment we touch.

"Oh God," she moans, gripping my hands tightly, closing her knees against my ears. "That feels so good, Sully. So good."

My nose nudges her clit as I press my tongue deep inside, extending it to its full length, using my lips to tease hers. Shelby's bucking against me like she hasn't had this in a long while, and as I concentrate on her clit, her whole body tightens.

Pulling back for just a few seconds, I lift my eyes up to watch her. "Everything good with you?"

"So good," she pants. "Don't stop, Sullivan. Please don't stop."

The way she says Sullivan, with a touch of pain and a whole lot of pleasure, is my fucking undoing. Frustrated, I growl, which causes her to spread her legs wider and rock against me as she searches for hers. Her nails dig into my fingers, but I refuse to let her go as her whole body goes taut, and she screams so loud I'm sure our neighbors hear her.

But I don't stop, even when she tries to close her legs to me. Even when she gets so wet I'm not sure where I begin and she ends. This is something I've craved for too long to let go with just one.

"Sully, you've gotta," she hisses through her teeth. "It's too much."

"Is it?" I mumble, letting her hands go.

Taking my palm, I spread it against her stomach, holding her down, using my thumb to expose her swollen flesh to my tongue. And again I go after her, knowing I can get number two if she just lets herself have it.

The high-pitch of her enjoyment starts to come back as I swipe my tongue up and down, flick her flesh with my thumb, and then I feel her again. Standing on my feet as quick as I can, I flatten my body against hers, do the same with my palm between her legs, and speak in her ear.

"There ya go. I knew you could be a good girl and give me another one." I rub her slightly. This time to bring her down, not build her up.

Lightly I nuzzle at her neck, feeling the sweat beading off her skin.

"Is there music playing?" She giggles. "I swear I can hear hymns."

I laugh along with her, but it quickly turns into a groan as her hand goes right to my dick, cupping it with a firm grip.

"Sully," she whispers in my ear, much like I did with her.

"Yeah?"

"It's my turn."

And when she takes my earlobe in her mouth, tugging with her teeth, I know I'm in for a ride I won't soon forget.

CHAPTER 11
SHELBY

EVERYTHING on my body shakes as Sullivan stands, dragging me along with him. I'm almost positive my brain is somewhere on the kitchen floor beneath us when he grabs hold of my hair, pushing me down to my knees.

His hand wraps around the back of my neck, before bringing it down, tilting my chin up. The gravel in his voice is enough to put goosebumps on every inch of my exposed skin.

His thumb rubs over my lips, both harsh and gentle at the same time. "If you feel uncomfortable, let me know. I'll never go further than you allow, but I warn you, Counselor, I can be overwhelming."

Sucking his thumb between my lips, I run my tongue around the tip before letting him withdraw. "Maybe I want overwhelming."

Eyes the color of coffee cloud with a desire I've never seen from any other man I've been with. Male hands answer with jerky movements unbutton his jeans and slide the denim along with his boxers to the floor.

"You ready?" The tone dark, sexual, and every bit as dangerous as the man himself.

Reaching out, I grab hold of the cock stretched to his belly button. With swift movements, I run my hand up and down, caressing the length, pausing as I get to the tip and collecting the fluid starting to gather at the tip. His groan is music to my ears, a small smirk plays against my lips before he's brought me flush with the counter and eased himself inside my mouth.

"Fuck yes."

The words are ripped out of his mouth forcefully. Grunted on a low tone that moves all the way through my body. Goosebumps sprout on my forearms, my nipples tighten, and moisture pools in my core. Though I just had mine, I could have it again easily – if he wanted to give it to me. His body weight presses against me, letting me know he controls this even though I'm the one giving out the pleasure this time.

"Your mouth is so goddamn wet, so hot." He talks through everything, and it's fucking glorious.

"Yes, swirl your tongue around the head. Suck deeper baby, harder."

My cheeks cave as I give into his requests. His fist in my hair pulls taut, causing me to lose my balance slightly. Reaching for him, I latch onto his ass, pulling him in tightly, digging my nails into his flesh.

"Let me feel it, Counselor. I'll wear the imprints of you all over my body any day of the fuckin' week."

The words are ripped from his throat, causing me to dig my nails in deeper. If he wants the badge of my passion, then I'll give it to him.

In and out he thrusts, my tongue bathing his erection in

saliva, helping the motion along. Making me feel powerful as he shudders with each press and pull. Never before have I felt this excitement, this arousal for giving someone else pleasure.

With my head tight against the cabinet, Sullivan leans over, hands gripping the lipped edge of the countertop, thrusting in earnest. It's an invasion I wasn't prepared for, but one I'll accept. For the time I've known him, I've never seen him lose control, and right now that's my main goal. To bring this man to his knees while I'm on mine.

"Ahhhh, Shelby," he hisses on a chocked groan.

I wish I could see his face, see exactly what I'm doing to him. Hoping like hell it's everything he does to me, and more.

"You feel so good."

With one hand, he lets go of the counter, bringing it down to cup my chin, bending slightly to close around my neck.

"I can feel myself deep in your throat," he whispers.

That's the understatement of the year.

Honestly, I can feel him in every part of my body. Each thrust echoes like one in my core, not just into my mouth. I rock against it, hoping to get satisfaction and to sate the desire coursing through my blood.

But I don't. It's a throbbing intensity all around us. An awareness I've not felt before. The feeling that this man is aroused by me, that I'm giving him something only I can.

"It's perfect," he growls. "Your mouth fits my cock so perfectly. I wanted this," he continues, so many secrets spilling from him. "From the first day I saw you. I knew, I knew you'd be different."

Different from what? I long to ask the question, but I'm

much too busy trying to keep up with what he's doing to me.

"There was something about you." He thrusts and grunts. "You seem real, when I haven't had real in so long."

Again I wonder who wasn't real. These are things I'm taking note of, making sure to ask him about when the time is right.

His thrusts slow down. "You okay?"

I make a noise in the back of my throat. Not a yes or a no, but a sound of contentment. As long as I'm giving him what he needs, I'm fine. My hands slip on his ass now that he's started to sweat.

"Do you know how hot you look right now, Counselor?"

I shake my head.

"Like a fuckin' porn star; you on your knees, naked, and letting me have my way with you. I bet your jaw is gettin' tired, huh?"

This time I nod, making a note that his southern accent starts coming out easier the more aroused he gets.

"Your knees are probably tired too, and I bet those lips of yours are red, tight as your pussy from where I've been stretching it with my cock."

This man – dear God this man – and his mouth. Nodding, I hum a yes as loudly as I can.

"You want me to come?" He toys with a strand of my hair.

"Mmm hmmm."

"Where? Down your throat? All over these tits?" He runs his calloused hand to my breasts, squeezing with his fingers.

I can't answer and he knows it.

"I don't need your input." He moves back up to wrap his hand in my hair. "I know exactly what I'm gonna do."

And that's when he goes after his orgasm hard. No reprieve, no taking it easy. The only thing I can do is breathe through my nose and concentrate on giving him the same kind of attention he gave to me.

Bringing my hand up to the base of his cock, I jack it as he presses in, pulls out, and repeats. I jack it hard, wanting more than anything for him to get off the way I did.

"Fuck, Shelby," he groans as he roughly withdraws from my mouth and shoots all over my chest and neck.

I close my eyes as I feel his essence drip down my body. The both of us are panting in the stillness of the room. When I slowly open my eyes, I see his sharp intakes of breath are highlighting the abs he has. How many hours a day does he work on them?

"How many hours a day do I work on what?"

I giggle. "Did I say that out loud?"

"You did."

"I was thinking about how many hours a day you must work on your abs for them to be as defined as they are."

He winks as he reaches down to run a hand along my jawline. "I had to do something to get rid of the sexual tension between us, Counselor. Hopefully now we can work out that tension together."

"I would love to." I look down at myself. "But first, I think I need to wash off."

He grabs my hand, pulling me up and to his body. The fluid from him smears against both of us. "Looks like I need a shower now too, huh?"

"Seems like it."

"Follow me, I happen to give good showers."

I laugh, grabbing hold of the hand he extends. "Oh, Sully, I just bet you do."

CHAPTER 12
SULLIVAN

"YOU'VE GOT a weird grin on your face."

"Am I not allowed to grin?"

"You're normally not this jovial."

"I always am when I'm with you, Ro." I throw my arm around my sister's neck, pulling her in tightly as we stroll through downtown Laurel Springs. It's cold today, our breath visible in the daylight. She snuggles in closely, allowing me to block the wind.

"Don't give me bullshit, Sully. What's got you smiling so much?"

We're in the square, and my eyes inadvertently go to Shelby's office. There's no denying it when Ro squeals, turning fully to face me.

"You and Shelby?"

"It's new." I hold my hands up, surrendering. She's a better interrogator than I am. "I'm not even sure what's going on with us."

"What do you mean? You should be positive about this woman."

Shoving my fists in my uniform pants, I shrug into myself. "If there's anything I've learned, I can't be positive until I know for sure."

"I'm sorry about things ended with you and Candice."

I haven't heard that name spoken or dared to speak it myself since I moved to Laurel Springs. It's weird to hear *Candice* roll off Rowan's lips. "Yeah, me too." I kick my feet on the sidewalk. "I thought we'd have a future."

And I had sorta planned on it. Which was stupid, I should've known. It wasn't the first time she'd broken my heart, but it'd damn-well been the last.

"Have you heard from her?"

Tilting my head to the side, I avoid her eyes. "She's left me a few messages. They're back together," I whisper. "He's still doing what he was before."

Her mouth hangs open. "Her and him are back together? Our brother is a fucking dumbass."

"Yeah. You can lead a horse to water, but you can't make it drink, huh?"

"Sullivan, I'm sorry."

"Yeah, me too." It's the only thing I can say. The only thing I'll allow myself to say on the matter.

"You can't let what happened with her fuck you over for life," she counsels me. "I mean, look how happy I am now."

My eyes sweep over her face. There's no doubt, she's happier right now than I've seen her in years. Given what she's been through – losing a baby, a marriage, and then meeting Cutter and moving here – she deserves every bit of joy she has. "It looks good on you."

"It looks good on you too. You should let Shelby in."

Rocking back on my feet, I roll my eyes. "It's not that

simple. We have a lot of chemistry, but it's never gone deeper than physical."

"Only because you won't allow it to go deeper. Open yourself up, bro. Life waits for no one. What if you lose your chance?"

It's a thought that crosses my mind more often than I care to admit. With the job I have, the times we live in, every day I go to work might be my last. I'm hyperaware. "I know." I pull a peppermint out of my pocket, before opening it and slipping it into my mouth. "I'm doing my best."

Her eyebrow quirks. "Are you? Are you, really?"

My radio chooses that moment to squeak. Saved by the fuckin' bell. "I gotta go." The adrenaline is already starting to run through my blood. It's part of why I love being a cop. Since the first hit of adrenaline I got with the job, I've never been able to give it up. Probably never will.

She reaches out, hugging me tightly. "Be careful, love you."

"Love you, too."

My feet beat a cadence against the sidewalk as I move toward my patrol car. There's a lot of traffic on the radio, and I'm trying to figure out what's happening.

"Possible domestic at thirty-five sixteen Laurel Court. Neighbors are reporting a large amount of yelling, and a crash. At the very least, they'd like there to be a welfare check."

"Do we know who lives there?" I ask, as I back out of the parking spot, flip my lights and sirens on, before driving toward the address.

"Property lists to Frank Gentry and wife. Doesn't show as a rental, assuming this is who you're going to find."

The name rings a bell. Other officers have been to this address a few times before. The wife hasn't ever wanted to press charges, though. Within minutes I arrive, Renegade is pulling up beside me with a squeal of the tires.

We each get out of our patrol vehicles. "How do I know this guy?" I ask. I'm still not completely sure where everybody belongs in Laurel Springs, especially when it comes to familial relations.

"He's the grandson of Widow Haley."

The other day at Shelby's office hits me like a brick. Mrs. Haley had been there to talk to her about something. I wonder if it entailed her grandson. As we approach the front door, I can hear them screaming at one another. Nothing that I can make out, but enough to give me an idea they aren't done with their argument. Using the butt of my flashlight, I bang on the door.

"Laurel Springs Police! Open up!"

The noise inside the house immediately comes to a halt. I eye Renegade, he eyes me back. Usually when things get very quiet, stuff can go wrong quickly.

"Laurel Springs Police! Open up!" I knock again.

I'm counting the seconds until I'll send a message to dispatch, asking if we can make entry to check welfare. I'm not the most patient in situations like this. My skin literally feels as if it could peel off my body. Right as I'm about to knock again, the front door opens and a man stands there, a blank look on his face.

"Can I help you?"

"We got a phone call that there might be a disturbance here. I need you to come out of the house. Who else is in there with you?"

"My wife." He gives me a smarmy smile. "We were having an argument. Normal married shit, ya know?"

"Not married." I give him a smirk back. "So I don't know."

"He does." He points to Renegade.

Ryan rocks back slightly. "Can't say Whit and I ever got the cops called on us, Frank." He does his best to keep his tone neutral.

"Don't have to when you're the police in this area, huh?"

Ryan and I exchange a glance. "Can you come on out?" I indicate him stepping over the threshold of the door with a finger. "We need to make a report since we were called."

His mood shifts quickly. "A report? Who the fuck called?"

"Someone who was worried. We can go over that later, but we need to verify your wife is okay."

There's a taut ribbon of tension between us. All my radars are going off, and it's obvious he doesn't want to speak to us about anything. Too bad that isn't going to fly with me.

"She's in the bathroom." He leans against the door frame, acting like he has all the time in the world.

"Can you go get her for me? I can't leave until I check on her."

His eyes narrow and his jaw tightens.

"If you don't, I'll see her another way." I fold my arms over my chest. "I'm not leaving here until I verify she's okay."

After doing this job as long as I have, you become very good at reading people. I'm reading him as being irritated that I'm still here.

"Montana!" he yells, not turning his head away from me, which means he screams right in my face. "This damn cop won't leave until he sees you're fine."

"You're used to intimidating people, aren't you?" I smirk.

"Most everyone I meet knows who I am." He shrugs.

I refuse to give this asshole the satisfaction. "I'm new in town." I cock my hip out to the side, placing my hand above my firearm. A little tip I learned my first year on the force in Paradise Lost. To most it gives the appearance of not caring, but for me and any other officer, it projects a *we mean business* attitude.

"Then you'll have to let me introduce myself to you once you ascertain my wife is very much okay."

"Lookin' forward to it."

He goes to shut the door, but I wedge my booted foot in before he can. Our eyes meet, and if looks could kill, I'd drop dead right here. Instead of saying another word, he turns around, presumably going to get his wife.

Renegade takes a spot behind me at my shoulder. "He's always had too high of an opinion of himself."

"Seems like he might need someone to take care of that for him."

Before we can talk anymore, a woman about my age is pushed through the front door.

"My wife," he bites out on a grimace. "Since you wanted to make sure she was okay, officer."

Keeping my gaze low, I give her a once-over, not at all liking what I'm seeing. Everything in my gut is telling me to get her away from him. "Ma'am, I'm gonna need to speak to you over here."

"Montana." The word is a threat.

"As an officer of the law," I cut him off, "I'm asking to speak to your wife. You stay here with Officer Kepler, and I'll be back to you ASAP."

Fuckin' asshole.

"My lawyer will hear about this."

"Great, I'll give you my name and badge number before I leave. Now." I gesture to the wife. "Over here if you please."

CHAPTER 13
SULLIVAN

I MAKE sure I don't turn my back on the two of them as I escort her toward my patrol car. When we get there, I lean against it so I can keep an eye on what's occurring over at the door.

"Can you tell me what happened here tonight?" I ask her carefully.

"Nothing." She folds her arms over her chest, effectively trying to shut me out.

With eyes that have watched too many other women in this situation, I see it all. The dried tears along her cheeks, the makeup she's tried to put on in a rush to conceal what's been done to her, the smeared mascara. The signs are all there, but there's one that gets me every time.

The eyes.

They always tell what the mouth won't.

The fear, sadness, isolation, and hopelessness of a situation they can't seem to change.

"You're safe."

"I know I am." She raises her chin slightly. "My husband would never hurt me."

I wonder how many times she's told herself those words as she cleans up her face, or puts a homemade splint on a sprain.

"Can you tell me what happened here tonight?" I try again, this time moving my eyes up to where Renegade is still dealing with her husband.

She sighs.

"Your neighbor called it in. We have to come and check it out. The best thing you can do is tell us what happened."

"And then you'll leave?"

It goes against everything I stand for, but I keep the promise in my voice. "Then I'll leave, as long as the law allows me to."

"Okay." She pulls her lip between her teeth. "He came home, and I didn't have dinner on the table."

It takes everything I have not to rage. "You didn't have dinner on the table?"

"Yeah." She pushes her hair back, and I notice a dark bruise on her wrist. "It's what he expects as the man of the house. I don't work," she says, trying to make an excuse.

"Did he put that mark on your wrist?"

She quickly pulls her long-sleeve shirt over where I've indicated. "Burned it making dinner. I was in a hurry," she continues.

"Because it wasn't ready when he got home?"

"Yeah," she whispers.

Her eyes are looking at me, but they aren't seeing a damn thing. It's almost as if she's rehearsed this so many times she can say it on autopilot. "What did he do when he realized dinner wasn't on the table."

She snorts. "It wasn't even on the stove."

Maybe I'm getting somewhere with her now. "What'd he have to say about that?"

"He yelled." Again with the vacant eyes. "He screamed and yelled. Threw a few things. Not to hurt me physically," she hurries out, like it makes a difference. "To hurt me emotionally. He broke my grandmother's serving platter."

What a fucking dick.

"Does he scream and yell a lot?"

She brings her hands up to her mouth, holding them over her lips. The material of her shirt is bunched between her fingers. She's pressing it all against her face, like she can either hold the words in, or she hadn't meant to let them out. "No more than anyone else. I should've had dinner done."

"Can't he fix it hisself?" I drawl as I lean harder on my patrol car.

"Obviously you don't know Frank Gentry."

No, I don't. But now I've made it my mission to find out everything I can about this piece of shit.

"ARE you surprised she didn't press charges on him?" Ryan asks as the two of us walk slowly back to our patrol cars.

We'd stayed at the Gentry residence for forty-five more minutes, trying to give her the time she needed to ask for help. But Montana, she hadn't. With her refusing to say Frank had hit her, and no evidence for us to use, we'd had to reluctantly let them go back to their night.

"Nah," I sigh. "All too often they don't choose to press charges until it's too late. I just wish there were something I could do for her. He seems like a real charming guy."

"Oh he is," Ryan laughs. "He sits on the board at the bank, but he only got the job because of his grandmother. Word around town says he's waiting for widow Hailey to kick the bucket. He's sure as shit he's gonna get her inheritance."

"Wouldn't it be funny if he didn't. What a punch in the nuts that would be."

Ryan shrugs. "It might make him worse. Men like him get worse when things don't seem to go their way."

Rubbing my hand across my chin, I think about what he's said. "Hopefully she gets out before he does."

"We can always hope," he sighs heavily, his shoulders slumping. "Either way, I'm going off-shift. Be safe out here, Sully."

"Will do, thanks for responding with me."

He grins before turning to walk toward his patrol car. "Always a pleasure, brother."

Getting into my own car, I watch Ryan drive away, wondering how he lets this stuff go. When I can't help someone, it eats at me. Sometimes for days, especially at night when I'm trying to calm down and go to sleep. After shifts like this, there's a need to expend some energy.

My phone buzzes loudly, causing me to reach over and grab it from the dash. On it, a text message from my soon to be brother-in-law.

C: We're doing a pick up game parks and rec. We need another person. Wanna join?

I've played pick up with Cutter and his EMT friends before. They're serious about it, and since I was a player in high school, I appreciate the gravity with which they take it.

S: I've got forty-five more minutes. Can y'all wait on me?

C: No problem, Devante's on his last run. We're waitin' on him too.

S: Then count me in. Sounds like a great time.

C: Cool, we'll see ya in a few.

This is another reason I wanted to move here when Rowan decided she was going to uproot herself from our hometown. Back there, I was known as the police chief's son, always regarded with looks.

Different kinds from different people.

There were those who thought I walked onto the police force without trying, there were others who thought I tried too hard, and even more who were completely indifferent to me. They refused to acknowledge me because they were scared they'd do something wrong and I'd report them to my father.

Moving to Laurel Springs has been a lifesaver.

In more ways than one.

CHAPTER 14
SHELBY

GLANCING AT THE CLOCK, I blow out a relieved breath when I see it reads five. This has been one of the longest work days ever. Probably because my night with Sullivan ran late.

A smirk plays along my lips as I think about what Sully and I did in his apartment. Today I haven't heard from him, but that's not completely unusual. More than likely he's been busy, just like I have.

My phone buzzes with a text, and I grab it as if it could walk away at any second.

K: We still on for coffee?

S: YES! Will be there ASAP, closing up the office right now.

Coffee with Karsyn. I can't believe I forgot.

Start thinking about Sullivan and everything else leaves my brain.

Quickly, I grab my briefcase and purse, throw my coat over my arm, and hurry to the door. I guess I'm lucky A

Whole Latte Love, the new coffee shop in town, is about a block from my office. Setting the alarm is second nature, and then I'm on the sidewalk. There aren't many people out and about today. As I shiver, I realize it's because of the coldness of the early evening.

My heels click against the concrete as I hurry to the coffee shop. Passing by The Café, I wave at a few familiar faces, and then put my head down into the wind and soldier on. When I get to the coffee shop, a gentleman holds the door open for me.

"Thank you."

"Not a problem," he answers. I watch as he ushers a little girl out in front of him, not much older than five.

For a moment I have a glimpse of Sullivan doing that to a kid who looks just like us. I have no idea where the vision comes from, but it doesn't scare me. Instead it brings a smile to my face, and a warmth to my heart.

"Shelby!"

My gaze goes directly to Karsyn when she waves to get my attention. "Hey." I wave back at her. "Sorry I'm late, I got caught up in work. Have you already ordered?"

"Less than five minutes ago. Go ahead, I'll watch your stuff."

Gratefully I put the things in my hands down, before grabbing my wallet out of my purse and joining the line for service.

"Welcome to *A Whole Latte Love,*" the barista greets me. "What can I get for you tonight?"

Browsing the board, my stomach growls when I see New York Blackout Cake. "A piece of the Blackout Cake and a cup of coffee."

"Cream and sugar?"

"Please."

"I'll bring it out to you in a few minutes." She indicates the small line behind me.

"Take your time, I'll be right over there." I point to where Karsyn is sitting.

"How's it going?" Karsyn asks when I get back to the table and have a seat. "I haven't talked to you in a while."

I shrug, folding my hands on the table. "It's going, waiting for business to pick up."

"It will," she encourages me. "It just takes time."

"I didn't realize how much it would take, and I'm trying to be patient, but I'm starting to get slightly worried. I'm starting to dip into my savings, and obviously that's not something I wanted to do within the first couple of years."

"You're a great attorney. Now that a few of the old-timers have retired, I'm sure you'll get more business."

"We can hope." I sit back from the table as our food and drinks are bought out to us.

"Do you know her?" Karsyn points to the woman behind the counter.

"Not really, I've been here a few times, but I don't know her name or anything, she's the owner if I remember correctly."

"She's gorgeous, wonder if she'd be up to the auction?"

I laugh. "Don't we have enough for that already?"

"We have more men than women, which is why I need you and her." She nods to the barista.

"Well then why don't you ask her?"

"Feels like I should get to know her first."

"Oh come on, Karsyn." I cut my eyes over at her. "This event is your and Whitney's baby. You'll do whatever it takes."

She's stopped from speaking as the other woman approaches our table.

"Here you ladies go."

"Thank you." I smile up at her after she puts mine and Karsyn's order on the table.

"No problem, thank you for being so patient."

I throw a pointed look across our coffee cups to my friend, before trying to engage the newcomer in conversation. "You're new in town, aren't you?"

She nods. "Moved here about six months ago and opened this place up."

"I moved here a little over a year ago," I offer. "Opened up my own practice. I'm an attorney."

Her eyes flare with understanding. "You're Shelby?"

"Yes." I grin. "Hopefully what you've heard is all good news."

"Mrs. Haley speaks very highly of you. She comes in a couple of times a week for coffee and a cinnamon roll."

"Mrs. Haley is a sweet lady."

There's a lull in the conversation and I legit stomp my toe on Karsyn's.

"Ouch!" She glares at me.

I glare back at her, before shifting my eyes to the coffee shop owner.

"My name's Karsyn," she says much too loudly, holding out a hand. "It's nice to meet you."

"Eden," she answers to both of us. "Probably should have introduced myself first. I'm still trying to figure out what's expected of me here."

Her accent isn't southern, which makes me wonder where she's from.

"I'm from the Houston area, how about you? You don't sound like a southern transplant."

"Chicago," she answers quickly. "The cost of living down here is cheaper, and allowed me to open without a bunch of loans."

"How would you like to get involved with the community?" Karsyn presses on.

"It would depend in what way."

"Have you heard of the LSERT?"

Eden nods. "Yeah, a few members come in here, and I did an order for your last meeting."

"You made those cookies?" My stomach growls just thinking about them. They were to die for.

"Yeah." She ducks her head in embarrassment.

"They were amazing. When Devante walked in, I could smell their goodness before I ever saw it."

"He was helping me out." She shrugs. "Business was kind of slow until he did that."

"I sympathize. It's hard, especially not being from here. But damn girl, keep baking like that and you'll have customers beating your door down."

Her caramel colored skin brightens enough at the cheeks to show a blush. "That's the plan."

"Good plan." I take a drink of my coffee.

"What would I be doing to help out?" She turns her attention to Karsyn.

"We're having a charity auction to raise money for the LSERT."

"Oh, I can donate some food and gift certificates."

"That would be great." Karsyn grins. "But not exactly what I was thinking. See..." She crosses and recrosses her legs, a sign she's nervous. "We're having a bachelor/bachelorette auction, and we need a few more women. Would you be willing to auction off a date with you?"

"Do you think anyone would mess with all these people connected to cops?" I'm quick to assure her. "This, after all, is to benefit the LSERT. They're too scared to want to do anything nefarious."

"It's the perfect way to get to know people in town," Karsyn adds. "And we can vouch for almost everyone. Live here long enough and you'll get to know them all."

I can see her weighing the pros and cons in her head. Given the way her eyes brighten up, I think she wants to do it, but something is holding her back.

"I'm doing it," I speak up. "It's for a great cause. I work with the LSERT and I can vouch for the good work they do. So does Karsyn. The money we raise with this event will go a long way toward community policing and helping to keep power on for residents during the hot summers."

"That's something I haven't dealt with yet." She brings her bottom lip between her teeth.

"It's all about what we can give back to the community, and we do that in many different ways."

"So you're saying it would look good, for me as a new business owner, to participate."

Karsyn purses her lips. "What I'm saying is it could get you in front of the community in a way you haven't been yet, and perhaps get more business."

A slow smile spreads across Eden's face. "If you think it's a good idea, then I'm all for it."

"Great! I can drop off the information to you tomorrow. What time will you be here?"

"Open til close." She rolls her eyes in an exasperated

way. "I'm still looking to hire someone to help me out. Until then, it's me, myself, and I."

"Girl," - I stop to take a drink of my coffee - "I completely understand what you're saying. There's no rest for the wicked."

"Or the weary." She winks as the doorbell chimes, letting her know someone else has come in. "It was nice to meet you, ladies."

"You too." We wave at her before she goes to take her place behind the counter.

"She's nice." I watch her interact with her new customer.

"And gorgeous. She'll be an asset to the auction."

"You sound like we're a bunch of horses getting ready to run the derby," I complain before taking a bite of my cake.

"Speaking of horses. I heard you spent the night with Sully last night."

My cake goes down the wrong way as I realize what she's just said, causing me to hack and cough.

"Do you need the Heimlich?" She giggles.

I shake my head, coughing and wiping the tears from under my eyes. "Karsyn, I swear to God, one day you'll be the death of me."

"As long as I see that shocked expression on your face before you go, it will totally be worth it."

CHAPTER 15
SULLIVAN

"PASS THE FUCKIN' ball, Ransom." I hold my hands up, showing I'm open. He glances over at me, trying to find a place where he can do as I've asked. He's being double-teamed by Cutter and Devante.

"Whatcha gonna do now?" Cutter talks shit to his brother. "We're all on you like white on rice."

"Get a new analogy." He lobs the ball over his head, about as far from me as he can get.

Since they're both surrounding him though, it allows me to make a break for it, but so does Tank, who's on their team. I see him diving for it, so I do the same, knowing I'm taller than him and have longer arms. We hit the hardwood floor together, but I manage to tip the ball in favor of my team.

This will fucking hurt tomorrow, or maybe even tonight, but I can't deny how good it feels to get physical on the court. This is something I needed, especially after having to deal with Frank Gentry.

The two of us push ourselves up on shaky arms.

"You alright?" he asks, bending over at the waist.

"Fine, you?"

He nods. "Good save."

I laugh. "Way to make me work for it, old man."

"Fuck you, Sullivan."

Before we can say anything else, the game is back on this side of the court. My team is ahead by ten points, but that doesn't mean we stop playing. We play harder when they make another basket. I'm guarding Cutter, who makes a mistake, allowing me to swiftly steal the ball from his hands and breakaway from the group. I push the ball down the court, before I grab it in my hands and jump, slamming it into the hoop as I grasp the edges, hanging on.

"You would have to make a show out of a slam dunk," Cutter gasps.

"Maybe you need to up your cardio, that way you can catch me next time."

"Ask your sister, my cardio's just fine."

All the guys on the court make an *oohhhh* noise as Cutter and I get nose to nose against one another. "You're lucky I like you." I point my finger in his face.

"Don't point at me, Sully." He lifts his hand to swat mine down.

I don't know what happens, but I push him.

Harder than I mean to.

He stumbles, but doesn't fall. It takes him more than a few steps to regain his balance.

Immediately Ransom runs to his brother and Devante runs to me. "He's your sister's fiancé, let this go," Devante says, grabbing hold of my shirt, forcing me to look at him. "Things are heated because we're playing ball. Walk it off."

"My sister should be off-limits for trash talking," I yell, doing my best to fight him off, but Devante is much stronger than I give him credit for. He's easily holding my arms down to the side.

Ransom says something to Cutter. Whatever it is, it causes him to stop pushing against his brother. He turns around, putting his hands above his head, interlocking his fingers. When he turns back around, he comes over to me. "I'm sorry, that was out of line."

"It was," I agree. "But I shouldn't have pushed you."

"You're right, she'll stay off-limits for trash talking. It's been a rough day."

I reach out to shake his hand. "Rough day here too. We're cool, brother."

"You promise?"

"I promise." I pull him into a hug. "Now let's get this game over."

WHEN I PULL into the parking lot of my apartment complex, luck is shining down on me. Shelby is doing the same in her spot a few places away. Getting out, I wait for her. I've wanted to see her all day.

"Did you work out?" She eyes my tank top and gym shorts.

"My second favorite kind. I played a game of pickup basketball at the rec center."

She walks toward me, shaking her hips, letting them sway in the dim light bathing the parking lot. It's sexy as hell the way she carries herself. The way she tempts me with a little look, a small purse of her lips, or just the heat apparent in her green eyes. We're a hair's breadth apart when she stops. "What's your favorite kind of workout?"

Reaching out, I grab her by the chin, forcing it up slightly so I can see her face. "I think you know what my favorite kind of workout is, Counselor."

Heat flares between the two of us, but when she reaches out to grab my waist, I flinch.

"Are you okay, Sully?"

"Went down hard fighting Tank for the basketball. Knew I'd feel it either tonight or tomorrow."

She lifts up my tank top, whistling as she sees my sides. "You're gonna have a nasty bruise in the morning." Her fingers lightly graze the skin, causing me to shiver.

"Part of the game." I shrug like it's no big deal, but right now it surely feels like one.

"Why don't you come up to my apartment? I have that huge soaking tub. It'll do you good to relax those muscles."

"If I come up to your apartment is relaxing all I'm gonna do?" I raise an eyebrow at her, aware of how often we've been alone and how often we've ended up undressed.

"Your virtue is safe with me, Sully," she giggles, reaching out to take my hand in hers.

"I was worried." I lean down, kissing her softly on the lips. "Let me go get some clothes to change into, and then I will gladly use your soaker tub."

We walk in comfortable silence, holding hands until we get to her apartment. She drops my fingers and fishes around for her keys. "Don't take too long."

"Trust me, I want to get back to you as soon as possible."

Both the cop in me, and the man who's finding himself caring deeply for her, wait until she gets inside and hears the lock put back into place before I take the stairs to my apartment. Even I'm surprised at how quickly I'm taking them; I can feel just how bruised I am, but I want to get back to

Shelby. It's a need I'm not able to explain – this feeling of wanting to be close to her. I've never had it before.

In my past relationships I've not been the guy so caught up on his girl he wasn't able to have a life outside of her. But with Shelby? I find myself wanting to talk to her throughout the day. A phone call to ask how it's going, to see if anyone has displeased her.

This is all new territory for me, and it's scary. Because no matter how bad I thought my heart was broken before.

Shelby Bruce could ruin me.

"HOW OFTEN DO you soak in this thing?" I ask as I'm waiting for the water to fill the tub.

She shrugs. "Not nearly enough. It was honestly a big perk when I moved in, one of the plusses that had me picking out this apartment."

"I'm sure the cop car in the parking lot was one too." I smirk.

Reaching into the tub, she flicks water at me. "You didn't live here then, thank you very much. Anyway," - she rolls her eyes - "I had grand visions of buying one of those tray things, sitting in here every night after a long day and catching up on my computer work in complete relaxation."

"How many times have you used it?"

She grins bashfully, a tiny dimple popping out in her right cheek. It's almost so small I can't see it, and I'm not sure I've noticed it before.

"Three times."

"Three times? Counselor, we gotta work on that. Sure you don't wanna take a dip with me tonight?"

Her eyes meet mine before they move down to my waist where I'm bunching up my shirt in my fingers, getting ready to pull it up and over my head. She's still watching and I raise an eyebrow. "Little privacy, huh?"

"Sorry," she mumbles before turning away.

"Just kidding, Shelby, you can look all you want."

And look she does. She turns back to me, letting her eyes roam my body. She makes a visual feast out of me, and damn do I wish I had the energy to put the chemistry between us to good use.

"Anybody ever told you, you look too good to be true?"

I laugh, reaching down to take my shorts off. "No." I lean against the cabinet, pulling my socks off. "Can't say they have."

"Someone should have told you," she whispers.

"Someone did." I walk over to her. "You."

The moment between us ends with smiles on our faces.

"Get in," she instructs. "I'll wash your back."

It's heaven as I dip down into the bordering on hot water, but it's exactly what my sore muscles need. This tub is big enough for me to stretch out in. The steam rising up around me creates a hazy kind of dream-like state. Leaning forward, I let Shelby wash off my back, moaning when she presses hard to get the knots out of the muscles.

"You carry a lot of tension in your shoulders." Her breath tickles my ear.

"Always have, probably always will."

For what feels like hours she works on my shoulders and upper back. When she finishes, I'm jelly. "God, what did you do to me?"

"Hopefully made you feel good." She stands up from

where she's kneeling beside the tub. "You take your time in here. I'll go fix us something to eat."

Reaching out, I grab hold of her hand. "That's not why I came here, Shelby."

"I know." She smiles softly. "I didn't want to be alone tonight either. Eating dinner by yourself sucks, especially when you've found someone you like to eat with."

I didn't have to say a word, but somehow she understood. "Thank you." I pull her hand up to my lips, kissing it softly.

"No need to thank me, I like having you around."

"I like having you around too."

As I watch her leave the bathroom, I wonder how quick is *too quick*. When I decide I don't want to answer, I lay my head back against the tub, close my eyes, and relax with a smile on my face.

CHAPTER 16
SHELBY

AS I LEAVE THE BATHROOM, I chance another look back at Sully. He's already rested his head against the tub, and seems to be deep in his thoughts. I can't help but wonder who takes care of him, after he takes care of the rest of the world.

My heart speeds up to scary levels when I realize I want to be that person for him. It's the first time I've ever had those thoughts about someone else. I would have to have them during one of the most transitional points of my life.

Shaking my head, I walk to the kitchen, trying to figure out what I can make him for dinner. I haven't been grocery shopping in a while. I'm very much content with cereal and a banana for dinner more often than not, but I know that won't do for the man in my bathroom.

Rifling through the cabinets, I spot some rice. Pulling it out, I check the expiration date, because I'm pretty sure I brought this from my old apartment. Sweet, two months to go.

"He'll want something to off-set the carbs." I look behind me toward the bathroom. "A man who looks like that doesn't eat many carbs."

Throwing the freezer door open, I find one lone bag of broccoli I bought sometime when I planned on losing the ten pounds I gained when I moved here. "Hopefully it's not freezer burnt. God, Shelby, you have nothing here to impress anyone."

I'd be laughing if it wasn't the truth. At least I know I have chicken marinating in the fridge. It's what I was going to fix myself. If there's one thing I can do, it's marinate and bake chicken.

I quickly get it in the oven, along with the broccoli into the microwave and rice on the stove top. I'm assuming Sullivan's still in the tub since I haven't seen or heard from him. Making a mad dash for my bedroom, I take off my work clothes only to debate with myself about what to wear.

Normally I wear a tank top and shorts, but it feels exposed with Sullivan here. Even though we've seen each other naked, there's a part of me that wants to prove we can hang out with each other. That not every time we're in the same space, we have to act on this crazy lust we feel for one another. If all we have is lust, then what are we doing here?

Lust sizzles and fades.

Love and true feelings remain.

Sighing, I pull my hair back into a ponytail. It's not that I love Sullivan. I could, but not yet. There's still so much we don't know about one another. Secrets I haven't shared, and I'm sure there's plenty he hasn't either.

When I'm comfortably wearing a t-shirt and a pair of sweatpants, I move back into the kitchen.

I'm not prepared to see Sullivan standing there, waiting on me.

Damn does he look good in my kitchen.

For precious moments I don't make my presence known. I want to watch him, commit every tattoo and muscle to memory, to know exactly where each drop of ink begins and ends. Only those that mean something to him know these things. He's a notoriously closed book to most he meets, but the more I've hung out with him in the past year, the more he's opened up to me.

But it's in these quiet pieces of time, where I can admire him without him knowing. They show me more about the man than anything else can.

He's leaning against the counter, a soft smile on his face as his fingers move on his phone. Looks like he's opted for comfort too. Sweatpants hang low on his waist, a worn t-shirt covers the top half. It says *Paradise Lost High School Basketball*.

"Did you play?"

His head shoots up. "You're ninja quiet," he laughs.

"You were involved." I gesture to his cell phone.

"I'm being harassed by Karsyn to be a bachelor in your auction."

"You already agreed," I argue.

"I don't really remember agreeing."

Going to the oven, I open the door, before bending to check the chicken. While bent, I cast a glance over my shoulder. "Pretty sure you agreed."

His eyes are staring at my ass. "You stay like that, and I'll agree to anything you want."

"Then tell Karsyn you'll be auctioned off with me."

He puts the phone on the counter, crossing his arms over his chest. "Do I get to bid on you?"

My pulse speeds up. "If you want."

His tongue peeks out from between his lips, caressing them, leaving a trail of moisture behind. "Oh, I definitely want."

"Let's hope you're the highest bidder."

"Been savin' my pennies." He winks.

Clearing my throat, I straighten up, grabbing a potholder. "Chicken's done, and so is everything else."

"Let me get you something to drink," he offers. "What do you want?"

I drank with him last night, and I make it a habit not to drink two nights in a row. "There should be some sweet tea in there."

He finds it, putting two glasses on the counter, and pouring from the pitcher. "You like three ice cubes, right?"

"I'm impressed you remember that about me."

"Oh, Counselor, you'd be surprised. But why three?"

"Two isn't enough and four waters it down."

He chuckles, picking the glasses up and taking them to my living room. We've eaten together enough not to have any pretenses about me sitting at the kitchen table. I always eat on the coffee table in the living room. He sets them down, along with napkins and silverware.

"Is this enough for you?" I scoop the broccoli onto his plate.

"Perfect." He grins. "I'm surprised you had anything of the green variety in here."

"Once or twice I've thought about losing this extra ten pounds I'm carrying. Never got around to making that shit though." I point to the green stems on his plate.

"Don't." He grabs hold of my finger.

"Don't what?"

"You're perfect the way you are, Shelby. Don't try to fit into someone's asinine idea of what a woman should look like." He reaches down, his fingers circling around my hips. "I like something to hold on to."

"You never answered my question." I put my hands on his chest, wanting nothing more than to pull him closer. Instead, I settle for feeling his heart beat.

"What question was that?"

He tilts his head to the side, coming in for a kiss. This one is different from all the others. There's no edge of passion and lust to it. It speaks of comfort and ease. A gentle melding of two lives. When he pulls back, I reach up, wiping the moisture off his bottom lip.

"Did you play basketball in high school?"

"Oh." He tosses his head back slightly. "I did."

"Were you any good?"

He lets go of my hips, putting a hand over his heart. "You wound me. How can you ask me if I was any good? I mean shouldn't you assume I am?"

We grab our plates, walking to the living room. "If there's anything I've learned since becoming a lawyer, it's that I shouldn't make any kind of assumption. More times than not, it's going to be wrong."

"This chicken is phenomenal. What did you marinate it in?"

"It's a secret. My own recipe." I take a bite of the rice. "You still haven't answered my question."

"Alright, alright. I was captain my senior year, lettered, and even went to the state championship game. We didn't win."

"You still sound bummed about it."

"We had some shitty referees; they didn't like us because we were from a small town. They made some shoddy calls and they cost us the game by three points."

A thought runs through my head, and I have to say it out loud. "I bet you had plenty of girls offering to make it better for you afterward."

He coughs loudly on his drink of tea. "I can't believe you would think so low of me, Counselor."

"Oh give me a break."

We're quiet for a few minutes as we get busy eating. It isn't until I'm almost done and he is done that he leans back on the couch, holding his stomach, that he answers me. "It wasn't afterward. I had to ride the bus with my teammates. It was a few hours later in my Dodge with a bench seat. Head cheerleader."

"Somehow that doesn't surprise me."

"Because I was captain and she was the head cheerleader?"

I nod.

"Shoulda listened to the other guys on the team who'd been with her. She gave sloppy head, like almost bit my dick off. I'm sitting there trying to get it out of her mouth and she's clamped down. Worst experience of my life."

A snort works its way out of my nose as I imagine a high school aged Sullivan trying to get his dick out of some girl's mouth.

"You laugh, but I was scared to death."

"Of what?" I giggle.

"I had fuckin' teeth marks. Teeth. Marks. I wasn't sure I'd ever be able to get it up again. That's dangerous for a seventeen-year-old guy who'd only had sex three times at that point."

"Poor thing."

"Yeah, poor me. I didn't let another girl go down on me for two years after that."

"You had blowjob PTSD?"

"Fuck yeah, I did."

We're both done with our meals, so I gather the plates, still giggling as I get up.

"What are you doing, Shelby?"

"Cleaning up our mess and then we can watch some mindless TV?"

"Uh uh." He shakes his head. "You cooked, I clean."

"I invited you, not so that you'd clean up, but so you could keep me company. I have a dishwasher."

"Then I'll gladly put these in the dishwasher. You go on over there and find us something to watch."

Instead of following him to the kitchen, I go back to the couch and grab the remote before sitting down again. Turning on the TV, I click the correct button for Netflix, and shuffle through the shows I've been watching. There, hidden at the end, is the one we've been binging.

It's our little secret.

We still have a few episodes to go and I can't wait to see how this show ends.

Sullivan comes back over, grabbing the blanket off the back of the couch, and lies down, holding his arms open for me. "C'mon in here. I gotta find out if Carole really killed her husband or not."

I giggle as I drop down beside him, snuggling up to his chest. He pulls the TV remote off the coffee table and goes to press play, but right before he does, I giggle-whisper. "Killed her husband, whacked him."

He laughs along with me, and as I press myself fully into his body, I let my mind imagine.

That this is where we'll be years from now. After spending time like this with Sullivan, I can't imagine ever letting him go.

CHAPTER 17
SULLIVAN

"WE WERE out at the Gentry's again last night." Ransom throws some paperwork onto my desk the next morning.

"Did she press charges?"

He gives me a look. "What do you think? She's scared to death of that prick, and he fucking gets off on it."

"This is the part I hate about being a cop." I pick up the papers he dropped. "You can want to help people all day long, but until they're ready to accept it there's not a goddamn thing you can do."

"I know, it's a bitch."

"Is this for the auction?" I'm flipping through what looks to be a consent form.

"Yeah, Whitney was over at the house yesterday, and apparently my job in helping with this fundraiser is doing all her paperwork delivery."

"I mean she does watch your kid," I remind him.

"She does, but she's the grandparent. It should be her honor."

A laugh-sigh breaks through my mouth. "You think real highly of yourself, don't you?"

"Hey, if I don't, who else will? Be sure to fill that out, stick it in my box, and I'll take it back to her."

"I'll stick it somewhere," I mumble.

"I heard that. You're the one who agreed to do this."

"I wouldn't say I agreed, so much as I didn't say anything and it was taken as agreement."

"Ole Shelby steam-rolled you like an asphalt paver. Welcome to my world, where all the women tell me what to do and I ask no questions. Questions get you in trouble. The best thing to do is just nod and smile."

"Is that famous Ransom advice?"

"It's Ransom advice, not sure I'd call it famous. Anywho, we're out." He makes a noise for Rambo, who gets up immediately to follow him.

"Be safe." I wave after them.

Turning my attention back to the packet of paper, I shake my head. There's a damn questionnaire. Do people really need to know this much shit about us? I stop reading when I hear someone clear their throat over me. Glancing up, I grin. "Sis, what are you doing here?"

I'm always excited to see Rowan, but she doesn't visit me on the job too often.

"Made apple pie for Cutter, and thought I'd bring you a piece."

My stomach growls loudly as I look down at the saran-wrapped plate she carries. "Oh my God, thank you."

"I have to admit, it's slightly to see how you're doing too, since you haven't answered my last three texts."

"I've been busy," I defend.

"With Shelby, I'm sure."

I can't deny it. "We've been spending time together."

"I'm happy for you, Sully, so happy, but please remember to let me know you're alright. I worry."

Standing up, I open my arms, pulling her into a tight hug. "Remember I'm older, I should be the one worrying about you."

"Age has nothing to do with it," she mumbles into my chest. "I'll always be scared when I know you're out protecting the people of Laurel Springs."

"You don't need to."

"But I will."

I let her go. "I wish I could stay here and chat, but I have to hit the street. Come see me soon?"

She rolls her eyes. "I'm the one who showed up here, you can come see me."

"Sassy as always."

"Love you, bro."

"Love you too."

Shelby

"NOW, Mrs. Haley, I need to verify this is what you definitely want. There's some paperwork for you to go over and sign. This basically says you are of sound mine and no one is forcing you to make these changes."

She leans forward, grabbing hold of the pen I've set down for her. Alert eyes skim the pages, before she signs her signature with a flourish.

"How will Montana know, once I'm gone?" Her voice cracks as she asks the question.

No one likes to think of their mortality, and given how

frail Mrs. Haley is, she's not too far from the end of her journey.

"That's my job. If anything happens to you, I probate the will. You don't have to worry about it. I'll make sure your wishes are carried out."

She sighs, almost with a touch of relief. "I've worried about this since they found the cancer. I can't tell you how much this means to me, Shelby."

"It's what I'm here for," I remind her.

"Either way," - she reaches into her pocket book - "I brought something for you. I want you to know I went to five lawyer's offices before coming to yours. None of them believed me to be of sound mind and tried to talk me out of changing my will. I know it's because of their connections with Frank."

She's given an opening I've always wanted to ask about. "What exactly does Frank do?"

Her tone is weary. "He does many things. He's on the city council, is on the board of directors at the bank, and at this moment he's blindly running Haley Corporation into the ground. I can't do anything about what he's doing with the bank or city council, but I can stop him from bankrupting our family business."

"No one stops him?"

"Back when my husband made his will, there wasn't thought to give businesses to the women of the family. We didn't have a son, so our grandson seemed like the obvious choice." She shrugs. "But he's grown too comfortable in his position. Instead of increasing our net worth, it's dropping. The money I'm giving Montana is money that was put in a trust; Frank's never been able to touch it. Which is why he's going to be angry when he finds out I've willed it to her."

"I'm sorry you've had to deal with this."

Her eyes are defeated, like she knows this is a last-ditch effort to make things right in her life before she goes. I can't imagine being this close to death and trying to wrap up pieces of a life I spent years creating, praying that I'm able to keep my accomplishments out of the Devil's hands.

"I should've dealt with it before now, but I wasn't strong enough. I refuse to give him what he wants. Not after I've seen how Montana has suffered. She deserves better, and I can give her that. If it's the last thing I do, she will be taken care of."

There's a part of me that almost tells her it's probably going to be the last thing. Mrs. Haley is frail, her voice husky and hoarse at the same time, and her eyes aren't bright. They're resigned.

She knows this is her Hail Mary.

"I'll make sure all your wishes are kept, Mrs. Haley."

"I know you will, which is why I want to give you this."

I reach forward to grab what she's holding out to me. It's a check for ten thousand dollars. "Mrs. Haley, this is too much," I protest, looking down at it.

"You were the only one to believe I knew my own mind, Shelby. It's my way of saying thank you."

"The words are good enough for me."

"Not for me." She reaches in, covering my hand with one of hers. "I lost my husband, my daughter, and in some aspects, I've lost my grandson. He's not the man he should be, and he's never going to live up to the expectations we've had for him. The best I can do is take care of Montana and thank you properly for what you've done. Please accept this gift, Shelby. It pleases me to be able to give it to you."

I don't know what to say or how to respond, so I smile.

Lord knows I need the money and it'd be foolish of me not to bank this for the real hard times that may be coming up. "Thank you, Mrs. Haley. It's been a pleasure working with you."

"You too." She puts her purse in her lap. "Now that I'm sure all of this is taken care of." She points to the papers in front of me.

"It'll be filed with the courthouse as soon as I leave here," I assure her.

"Good, good. I must let you know, I'm going into Hospice care in the morning."

My heart drops.

"Oh, Mrs. Haley, I'm so sorry."

"Don't be, you've given me peace of mind no one else could. It's everything I wanted before I leave this earth. I can go with my conscience clear."

I'm more emotional than I should be. As she stands, I get up and go around the desk. On impulse I envelop her in a hug. She holds me back tightly.

"If you need anything, Mrs. Haley, please let me know."

"I will, Shelby. Thank you for making this so easy on me."

I want to say more, but I'm at a loss with what words to use. What do you tell someone whose about to enter the last stages of their life?

"Will you make sure someone tells me." I fight back tears. "When it happens? Not because I need to know for probate reasons, but because I think of you as a friend."

She smiles graciously. "I sure will."

When she turns to leave, I don't know what else to say. What is there to say? Walking with her to the door, I open it for her, and watch as she makes her way to her car. Mrs. Haley is the only person I know who has a driver.

He gets out when he sees her coming. I look as he opens the door for her, escorting her inside. When he glances over at me, I give him a wave. He gives me one back, and even from where I stand, I can see the sadness in his eyes.

Both of us know.

She doesn't have much time left.

CHAPTER 18
SHELBY

WHEN I GET HOME, I don't see Sully's patrol SUV, which means he's probably still on-shift. Until right now, I didn't realize how much I look forward to seeing him at the end of a stressful day.

Reaching in, I grab my briefcase and drag myself up the stairs to my apartment. Going into an empty living room is not what I want to do, but it's the life I have right now.

It's nights like these I wish I had the life of most of the friends I've made here in Laurel Springs. Everyone is married with kids, or fixing to get married.

They're settled.

And I'm not.

All the plans I had for myself seem to have never come to fruition, except being a lawyer. I love my job and I'm incredibly proud of what I've done, but none of my personal goals have been achieved.

I'm not married, no kids, not even a prospect. Granted, Sully and I are getting closer, but who knows how close we'll get. Who knows how far it'll go – it's just as likely we'll burn hot and fizzle out - as is it we'll stick it out for the long haul.

After I turn on the lights, I look around.

Damn, I don't want to be here.

But what can I do? Where can I go?

Picking up my phone, I log onto Facebook to see what the people in my old life are doing when I'm hit with a targeted ad for the bar in town. According to it, tonight's ladies' night, and just like that, I know exactly what I'm going to do.

Sullivan

"ARE you gonna tell me those aren't your pants?" I ask the teenager in cuffs as I search his jeans. I've already found paraphernalia, and I'm pretty sure I'll find more.

"Swear to you. They aren't mine."

If only I had a dollar for every time someone lied about their clothes. I wouldn't be doing this job anymore. I'd be living on some deserted island in the Caribbean.

"The problem is they're in your possession."

"Come on, man, my mom is going to kill me."

There are people I wish I could cut a break, then there are people who I can instantly tell will never change. I'm not sure who this kid is yet, but I do know if we take the chance to scare him now, we might be able to set him on a better path.

"Are your parents home?" I ask, taking his wallet out of his back pocket.

When I shake it, nothing falls out, which is good for him. I grab his ID. He's only sixteen.

"She's at work," he mumbles.

"She work the night shift?" I was supposed to have gotten off at four, but here it is, eight and I'm still on.

"Yeah, at the factory over in Calvert City."

Chances are they're working overtime, and this kid has been left on his own while they try to get as much money as they can to make ends meet. I hate to bring trouble to their doorstep, but kids make bad choices and sometimes parents have to pay for it.

"We'll have someone call them when we get to the station. Put your hands behind your back like you're praying."

"I don't wanna go to jail," he argues, tensing up.

Truth is, I don't wanna take him to jail, but I have no choice. There are times when what I have to do can be a fork in the road for their futures. I'm praying this one makes the right decision.

"Relax, otherwise you're going to hurt in these cuffs. I'm sorry, but I have to do my job. I'm taking you in on the paraphernalia, and the smell of marijuana. The K-9 is on his way since you didn't give me permission to search."

Taking hold of his arm, I drag him over to the curb, helping him to sit down. He's quiet as he looks at me with hate-filled eyes.

"Is this the first time you've been pulled over?" I ask, trying to make some sort of connection with him.

He sighs. "Yeah."

"It's too bad for you that you had a one-hitter and the car smells like weed. Look." I kneel down to where I'm eye-level with him. "Everybody's gonna experiment now and again. Maybe you need to blow off some steam. We all gotta do that too, but the fact of the matter is, weed is a drug. It's illegal here in the state of Alabama, and as a cop, I have to uphold the law."

"It's a stupid law," he mumbles.

While I agree, it's better for me to keep my mouth shut. "It is what it is, kid. We've all been here before. You're not the first, you won't be the last."

"Is that supposed to make me feel better?"

"No, it's supposed to help you realize this is a turning point in your life. Where you decide to go from here makes a difference."

He rolls his eyes. "You're not my dad."

"Where is your dad?" I ask as I lean against my cruiser.

"Don't know." He shrugs. "Didn't stick around, but it doesn't matter."

There's something about this kid that makes me want to help him, makes me want to help him believe things can change, that not everyone who has a rough start in life has to settle.

"It does matter," I argue. "Don't you want to prove him wrong? Doing this shit isn't going to do that."

"How's he going to know?"

"Him knowing doesn't matter, it's what *you* know." I push off the car, lean down, and point to his heart. "It's what you know in here that matters. You'll know you're better than him. The best version of you. Someone you can be proud of. Don't do what you think he might suspect of you, do what you know is right."

"It's easy for you to say."

"Don't tell me what's easy. My dad? He was the Chief of Police. Any little thing I did, he knew about. There were no free passes, there was no learning from your mistakes. They were moments in time that should have been learning experiences, but they weren't. Instead, especially for me and my brother, they were chances for punishment, and the silent treatment."

"At least he cared."

"He did," I admit. "But at the time, it felt a lot different. It took me getting older and seeing it from what I imagine his perspective was."

"Am I supposed to feel sorry for you?"

"No, what I want you to realize is when you get older your perspective is going to change." I have a seat next to him. "It's your decision how it changes. Is this going to be the only mark on your record? Or is it going to be the first of more to come? It's all up to you, my man," I clap his shoulder as I see Ransom pulling up with Rambo. "Make your choice wisely."

Ransom and I nod at one another when he gets out of his SUV, opening the back door for Rambo.

"Thanks for coming." I get up and walk over to him.

"Been a slow night," he sighs. "Kinda wish I was home with the wife and kid."

"Whipped."

He chuckles. "Fuck yeah I am. This the car?" He points to the car in front of us.

"Sure is. Let me know if you find anything."

I stand back to let Rambo work. He's one of the most loved members of our force, and I enjoy watching him whenever I can.

"What's he going to do?" the kid asks.

"He's gonna tell me if we need to search your car."

"Man, this is fucked up."

I ignore what he's saying, watching Rambo to see if he alerts. When he does, Ransom and I look at one another. He puts Rambo up, telling him what a good boy he is. He slowly walks over to where we are, covering his hands with gloves.

"So," - he stops in front of us, looking down at the handcuffed teenager - "my dog alerted, which gives me permission to search your car. Is there anything you want to tell us about before we start looking?"

"I have nothing to say to you."

He's defiant, and I wish he'd understand all we're trying to do is help him.

"It's your decision." I shrug, motioning over to Ransom. "Go ahead and search it."

"This could have gone so much easier, all you had to do was tell us what you have. Neither one of us enjoy having to search. I hope you know that."

"Don't lie." He glares up at me. "You get off on this. All law enforcement does."

"No, we don't. Maybe some do, but we don't."

"Yeah, that's what they all say."

"Sullivan, come here for a sec."

Shaking my head, I go over to where Ransom stands, the back door of the car open.

"Yeah?"

"He's got four baggies of weed in here. Read him his rights, he'll be going to jail tonight."

"Those aren't mine," he screams as he hears what we're saying.

Instead of rising to his irritation, I go over and start the process of arresting him.

No matter how much I don't want to do it.

CHAPTER 19
SHELBY

"THANKS FOR COMING WITH ME," I yell at Karsyn over the sound of the live band playing at the only bar in town. She was the first person I thought of when I saw the ad on my social media. Lucky for me, Tucker is working tonight, so she's my wing woman.

She takes a drink of her beer, a grin breaking out across her face. "No problem. I haven't been out in a while, seemed fun. I hate sitting at home, waiting for Tucker to come home. My imagination runs wild at all the things that could wrong. Just wait until you and Sullivan get further into it. You'll know the fear too."

I almost tell her I already feel the fear. Sometimes I wait to see him pull into the parking lot at the end of a shift, just so I can make sure he's okay.

We're standing next to the pool tables when we hear someone speak. "Ladies, would you like to play?"

"Not me." Karsyn shakes her head. "I'm not very good."

"What about you, blondie?"

My eyes move over the body of the man speaking to us.

He looks harmless, and I don't get any weird feelings from him. As an attorney I've always trusted my gut. Tonight it says this guy just wants a little friendly competition.

"What are we betting?" I wink at Karsyn.

He reaches into his jeans pocket, pulling out a single bill. "One hundred bucks." He slams it down on the side of the pool table.

"Didn't bring my purse inside, but if you win, I'll run out and get it."

"What do you mean *if* I win?"

I shrug. "Maybe I have a few tricks up my sleeve."

He chuckles. "I'd love to see them."

Going over to the wall, I grab a pool cue off and chalk the tip. "Can I go first?"

"Of course, you're a lady."

Many people have underestimated me in my life, and it looks like this guy will be added to the long list. Leaning down I give the cue a hard push and break. Nothing goes in, but I set up my first shot beautifully. "I call stripes. Number one in the left side pocket." I point to the one I'm going to make.

It goes in with an ease I'm sure this guy didn't expect.

"Good shot." His eyes show suspicion he's been had.

"Was it really?" I reach down to take a drink of my beer.

Karsyn snickers as her eyes meet mine. She had no idea about what I can do with a pool cue, but it's obvious she's enjoying herself.

"Three ball right there." I nod to indicate the corner pocket, before smacking the ball hard.

"Go, Shelby!" Karsyn yells in excitement.

Ten minutes later, I miss my first shot. It's one I didn't

mean to; I took my eyes off the ball for a split second when Sullivan walked through the door.

"What's he doing here?" I ask Karsyn after I stand up and move back from the pool table.

She makes a noise that says she doesn't know either. I do my best to pay attention to what's happening on the table, but instead I'm watching Sullivan as he walks across the room.

It's nice observing him when he doesn't know I'm looking.

The man walks into a room like he owns it. His long legs eat up the floor, and while part of me wishes he'd look over and see me, the other part just wants to keep watching.

He slides up to a table full of guys, and I notice a few local first responders. A waitress comes over, and even from where I stand, I can see the way she runs her eyes up and down his body. She's definitely interested.

"Would it be awful if I went down there and gouged her eyes out?" I ask Karsyn before I take another drink of my beer.

"No, girl, I'd think the same thing."

"Shit, it's your turn," the guy sighs as he back pedals from the pool table.

Since I wasn't paying attention, him cursing causes me to look at what's going on back at the pool table. Before I was all about trash-talking and doing the best I could to get his mind out of the game. Now I wanna get done, go down there, and claim my man.

Doesn't matter that we haven't claimed each other before. Right now I'm ready to tell the entire world he's mine, even if the entire world is Laurel Springs, Alabama.

Sullivan

"WHAT'S GOING ON UP THERE at the pool tables?" Caleb asks as he leans over so he can be heard.

This bar is loud, which I'm not entirely used to. In Paradise Lost the bar I liked to go to was mostly outdoors. The live music reverberates off the walls, along with the voices of the patrons.

It's a scientific fact that drunk people talk louder than they need to. Those of us who aren't toasted have to try extra hard to hold a conversation. Looking over to where he's pointed, I crane my head up and around. It's then that I see a woman bent over the pool table.

I would know the curve of that ass anywhere.

"I'll be right back, I think I know who that is." I push away from the table, reach down to grab my glass of beer, then walk to where the crowd has gathered.

"Fancy meeting you here."

Turning to my right, I see Karsyn.

"Hey." I reach out, giving her a one-armed hug. "That's Shelby, isn't it?" Her back is still to me.

"Yeah, she's wiping the floor with this guy who greatly underestimated her."

My eyes eat her up as she walks to the other side of the table. With her pool cue, she points. "Eight ball in the left pocket."

"You'll never make it." One of the guys standing around laughs at her.

It's going to be a difficult shot. She has to hit it off the opposite side and ricochet it into the pocket.

"Bet you I do." She grins.

Her eyes meet mine and I flash her a smile. She gives me

a slight finger wave, as if to tell me when she's done handing this guy his ass, she'll be able to get with me.

Leaning over, she eyes up her shot, and I do my best not to let my gaze drift down to the cleavage sticking out of her shirt. I'm sure every other guy is checking her out to, but this woman? She's mine.

Mind. Body. Soul.

She's mine.

Right before she takes her shot, her gaze flits up to mine and she fucking winks. Which goes straight to my dick. I swear when the crack of the balls knocking against each other rings out, there's a jolt that goes through my body. Everybody waits to see if it goes into the pocket, and when it does, the whole crowd erupts.

I can't help it, I run over to where she's standing and grab her up at the waist, swinging her around.

"You don't even know what I won," she giggles, wrapping her arms around my neck, her legs around my waist.

"Doesn't matter." I shake my head. "Any win for you is a win for us, babe."

Her eyes soften before she leans in to fuse our mouths together. We haven't been public yet, but that's all changing in this instant. Her fingers dive into the back of my hair, holding the kiss longer.

There's wolf whistles and shouts of encouragement before we break apart.

"Here's your winnings. Good game." A man hands her a hundred dollar bill.

"Thanks for being a great opponent. It was fun playing against you."

I let her down, twirling her around once or twice before allowing her feet to hit the floor.

"Where'd you learn how to play like that?"

She grins, looking up at me, her eyes dancing in the dim light. "It's how I paid for law school."

I throw back my head, laughing loudly. "You were a pool shark?"

"A girl's gotta do what a girl's gotta do."

Easing my hands into the back pockets of her jeans, I pull her close again. Leaning in, I speak in her ear. "Come on down where I am and join us."

"Are you sure? We haven't exactly been open to everyone about what's going on between us. We haven't told anyone really. Are you okay with going down there and being the talk of the town?"

"As long as I'm being linked with you, I'm completely okay with that."

"Same here."

I grab her hand, leading her down to where I had been sitting before. Pulling an extra couple of chairs over, we rearrange ourselves so Shelby and Karsyn can sit with us. It's hard not to notice everyone looking at us from their seats at the table, especially when I put my arm around her neck, pulling her in closer.

The waitress comes back, and Shelby scoots in, practically on my lap.

"Do you need anything?" the waitress asks.

"No, I'm good," I answer, not tearing my gaze away from Shelby.

She doesn't ask anyone else if they want anything.

"I'd like another beer, please," Shelby pipes up, holding her empty bottle. "If it's not too much trouble."

"I'm about to go off shift." She ignores her request.

"I bet if my boyfriend here asked you for a beer, you'd

move heaven and earth to get it. Sorry you got the wrong idea earlier, but he didn't come here looking for another woman, honey."

"Yeah." I grin, grabbing hold of Shelby's thigh. "I got the one I want and need right here."

CHAPTER 20
SULLIVAN

"IT'S hot as fuck in here." Cutter runs a hand through his hair.

The Laurel Springs Emergency Response Team isn't a small group of people, and Cutter's right - it's stifling. When we have a meeting with all of us, it's obvious we need a different space.

"They must have the heat on."

"On the day it's almost seventy degrees outside," Cutter bitches.

"It was chilly up until today. Who pissed in your Cheerios?" I give him a look.

"Dude, I have been up for thirty-six fucking hours," he grumbles.

"Why so long?"

He rolls his eyes. "Somebody called in and we couldn't find anyone to take the spot. It's not like we can run ambulances without EMTs, so I had to stay."

"Don't act like you're the only one," a voice says from the other side of Cutter's body.

Moving forward slightly, I glance by him to see who's talking. "Hey, Devante." I reach out my hand to shake his. "How you doing?"

"Tired as fuck, just like Cutter, but if you ask him, he's the only one working more than a twelve-hour shift."

"Don't invalidate my feelings," he argues.

"Jesus," I sigh. "Nobody's invalidating your feelings, but you're not the only one who's pulling crazy shifts. Every department has issues at one time or another. You're not a special snowflake."

"You two suck."

"Oh, that's a mature come back."

If looks could kill, I'd be dead. Cutter's mean mugging hard. Instead of standing with him and Devante, I give them a wave. "See y'all."

Right as I'm walking by the door, I get a whiff of coconut and strawberries. It's gotta be Shelby about to come in. Opening it, I see her surprised face.

"Hey." She grins. "Are you on gentleman door duty?"

Leaning in I cup a hand around her hip, before kissing her on the cheek. "Only for you, and maybe Ro if she was here."

"I'll allow it."

This time she tips her face up to mine, placing a chaste kiss on my jawline. Except nothing with us is ever really chaste. Putting my arm around her waist, I direct her to the other side of the room.

"Is there any reason you're having us sit as far away from Cutter as we can get? I thought you two were close."

My eyes are drawn to her legs as she crosses them. The skirt she wears inches up farther on her thighs, showing more of the tights covering the limbs.

"Hey," she giggles. "Eyes up here."

My cheeks heat with embarrassment. Not because I was caught looking at her the way I was, but because we're out in public and she may not want this much PDA.

"Sorry." I shake my head to remind myself where I am.

"It's okay. It's nice to know you like looking." She leans in, her lips barely touching the outer edge of my ear. "Maybe later I'll wear these and nothing else."

A groan rips its way from my throat. "I hate that I have to go back to work after this."

"That's the best thing about being your own boss." She laughs. "I get to make the hours. I coulda fit you in, but your loss."

I love this side of her, we don't normally get to tease one another. Our time together is limited and it's as if we don't want to waste it by saying words that aren't critical to our conversations. But this? It's nice.

"You have yet to *fit me in*, Counselor, but it's gonna be soon." I talk quietly so no one else can hear.

Her answer is a giggled whisper-hiss. "I can't believe you just said that!"

"Oh yes you can."

"Are you going to answer my question?"

"I thought I did."

"Why are you sitting as far away from Cutter as you can get?"

"Oh that question." I lean back slightly, putting my arm around her neck and stretching out my legs. "He's very annoying today; he's bitching about working extra shifts, and I didn't want to hear it. I'm pulling overtime too. In fact, the other night when you saw me at the bar, I had just worked fifteen hours on. He's not the only one, but you would think he was."

The way Shelby snuggles in next to me brings a smile to my face, and does crazy things to my chest. There's a warmth in there that I've never had. Even for women I've said *I love you* to.

"What if he's having an off day? We're all allowed, ya know?"

"You're so nice to be playing devil's advocate, but he does this shit all the time. He loves his job, but if it takes any of his and Ro's time together he gets super salty."

"I dunno." She shrugs. "That's kinda sweet."

I make a noise in the back of my throat. "It is, but we all know what we sign up for when we take these jobs. It's a lot of not being with our families when we want to be, and putting the good of the community in front of most things in our lives."

"Do you see yourself ever not being a cop?"

"No, it's the only thing I've ever wanted to be. Do you see me not being a cop?"

She shakes her head. "No."

"Is that okay with you? If this turns into something long-term? Could you live with that, Shelby?"

My heart pounds in my chest as I wait for her answer. Me being a cop has been a problem in more than one relationship I've tried to have. This one though? This one means more to me than any other one I've had. It feels like a lifetime before she answers.

Turning toward me, she leans in, her voice soft. "To be with you, I'll learn to live with it."

We might be in public, but I can't hold back. My hand cups her neck before delving up into her hair, tilting her face to give me room to take her lips. This isn't an easy kiss, it's a brand, a possession, letting anyone who may not know, this woman is mine. For long minutes, we get lost in one another, until I pull back, resting my forehead against hers.

"If you two are done, we can get our meeting started."

The room makes a ton of noise after Menace speaks. Hooting and hollering, making kissing sounds. Shelby buries her head in my neck.

I clear my throat. "Please, go ahead."

"Thanks for your permission."

"You're welcome." I grin.

He rolls his eyes, but I can see the smile playing at the corners of his lips. "Now that we've got the okay to get started, I wanna thank you all for being here today. We're here to talk about the fundraiser, so I'm gonna turn the floor over to Whitney."

I can hear Renegade whistle loudly for his wife.

"Thank you." She gives him a huge smile. "What we're going to do is a bachelorette and a bachelor auction. Sullivan," - she looks over at me - "when we were first talking about this, we didn't know the two of you apparently have a thing, so both of you are going to have to participate."

"Anything for the LSERT," I shout.

"Thank you! Plan on having the auction three weeks from today. We'll be doing it at the Laurel Springs Country Club. Thank you, Blaze, for getting us in."

"No problem, it pisses my mom off, so it's a win/win."

Whitney chooses to ignore what Blaze said. "You'll all need to be there an hour before doors open. I'm giving your supervisors the schedule. They've all agreed to let you off for the night. Does anyone have any questions?"

"What's our goal?" someone asks from the back of the room.

"As much money as we can," she answers. "We need some new water rescue equipment, and before we know it hurricane season will be here. As much as we can bank, we need to."

"Well," - Devante steps forward - "y'all can guarantee I'll be getting the most money."

"Ummm, excuse you," a girl standing beside Karsyn says. "I'm new to town, I'll get more money. I have the air of mystery around me."

They get into a small one-up match, before I turn to Shelby. "Who is that?"

"She's a new nurse at the hospital. Her name is Alisa. I'm not sure where she's from, but her and Stella know one another. She was at our last girls night out. She seems nice."

"Seems that lots of people are moving to Laurel Springs."

"We should know," she laughs. "We're new here too."

But it doesn't feel like it. If I'm being honest, Laurel Springs feels more like home than Paradise Lost ever did.

I can see myself staying here for the rest of my life, and I admit for the first time I can see Shelby being right by my side.

CHAPTER 21
SHELBY

"NO, NO, NO," I shout as my copier eats the paper I'm trying to copy. "Son of a bitch." I brought it from Houston, and it was on its last leg then. "I just need you to last a few more weeks," I beg it. In two weeks I'll be going to the Laurel Springs PD to write out wills for any of the officers who don't have one yet.

"Is everything okay in here?"

"I didn't even hear you come in," I tell Stella as I beat on the side of the damn machine.

"You were too busy yelling at the copier."

"It's lucky I don't throw it out the window," I groan. "What do you need?"

She has a seat on the couch in my office. "We're having a girls night out. Come join us, we've all had a shitty week."

"I am so there," I groan again when the copier eats the paper. "Fuck this thing, when are we leaving?"

"Right now." She laughs as I slam the top down.

"Let's go." I walk around my desk, grab my purse out of

it, and turn the open sign to closed. "Who all's coming?" I ask as we walk to the local Mexican food restaurant.

"I'm not completely sure, but there's definitely a group."

There usually is when we all get together. I'm so grateful to have met this group of people when I moved here. They took me in, and have been steadfast friends from the first day. Stella and I enter the restaurant and we immediately see our group. They're seated in the middle, already with chips, salsa, and margaritas on the table. They wave us over, and I go like I have a fire under my ass.

"What can I get for you?" the waiter asks as I take off my suit coat, hanging it on my chair.

"Queso and a strawberry margarita."

"Frozen or on the rocks."

"What the hell, give me frozen today. I'm gonna live a little."

Karsyn laughs. "Bring us a round of shots. If we're gonna live a little, we need to really do it."

"Something tells me we're going to need some designated drivers."

Stella takes a sip of her margarita. "Well since most of us know a police officer, I think we're good to go."

"If I call Tucker, telling him I need a ride home, I'm gonna never hear the end of it," Karsyn groans.

"Offer to blow him on the ride home," Stella says with a dead ass straight face. "Works every time."

"Oh my God," Karsyn laughs. "Is that what you do with Ransom?"

She grins. "I'm not one to brag, but it's never failed me yet."

"Have you done it in his patrol SUV?" I ask as the waiter puts my queso and margarita in front of me.

Everyone stares. "What? It's a question I have."

"It's a question I have too," Kels pipes up from where she sits.

Stella smirks, her eyes twinkling. "I may have."

"You either have or you haven't." I pressure her, grabbing a chip and dunking it into my cheese. "There's no may or may not. You started this discussion. Finish it."

"Okay." She takes a fortifying drink. "I have done it to him in his patrol SUV."

"Was he on patrol?"

"He was on a break, thank you very much."

"When?" Kelsea leans forward.

Everyone looks at her.

"What? I'm taking notes. It's hard to get time alone with two kids in the house, okay?"

Stella rolls her eyes upward. "It was when Keegan was a toddler. I'd taken him over to Mom and Dad's. I lied to them and said I had a couple of appointments, and they were going to keep him overnight anyway. Instead I went home and took a like four-hour nap. Ladies, I was *rested up* and ready to go."

"You look so excited about it, even now," I laugh.

"Because it had been months y'all, months. We'd been on separate shifts and even when we were home together both of us were so tired because of chasing after Keegan." She has a smile on her face. "Let's just say it was a good night."

We all giggle as she flushes read.

"What was so good about it?" Alisa asks. "Remember I'm new here. I haven't had a date since I moved."

Stella takes a fortifying drink of her margarita, and just

as she's about to launch into what she and Ransom did, our waiter comes back to get our orders.

He goes around the table, flirting with all of us, making us all laugh and blush.

"Do you ladies need another round?"

"Yes!" Stella yells. "We definitely need another round."

"You're not getting away with not telling us your story," Ruby reminds Stella.

When the new margarita is placed in front of her, Stella takes another drink, waiting for the rest of us to get ours. After the waiter leaves, we all lean in, waiting for Stella to tell us her story.

"Okay, so," she starts. "I'd taken my nap, and then I got up, shaved everything and did my hair, my makeup, and put on a sexy dress. It had a slit, and it was very low cut. I even put on some boots. I was ready."

"Over the knee boots?" Karsyn asks. "Like the type you could keep on during?"

"Yes, girl," she answers. "I'd made him lunch that night, so I asked dispatch to let me know when and where he took it, so that I could surprise him. Ransom is a man of habit. There's only a few places he takes lunch when it's not The Café. I was parked basically in the middle of all of them when dispatch called to let me know where he was."

She stops as our food is dropped off, and then we're all waiting for the rest of the story.

"How did he react?" Kels asks.

"When I pulled up, you could tell he was surprised. He had this cute little grin on his face, happy to see me during his shift. I walked over to the SUV, opened the door, and told him he probably wanted to secure his gun because I wanted him to fuck me."

"Oh my God," Alisa giggles.

"If any of you ask me about this later, I'm going to blame it on the margaritas and say you're cray, cray."

"Understood," Ruby says. "But you've gotta finish this story."

"He looked like he was about to stroke out, but when I grabbed him over his pants, he got with the program. He unholstered his gun and secured it, before getting out of the SUV and pressing me up against the back door."

"Tell me you wrapped your legs around his waist with those fuck me boots you had on." Alisa grins.

"Girl, you know I did," she laughs. I wasn't sure how we were going to do it, but he pulled me into the driver's seat and pushed it back as far as Rambo's cage would let it go."

"Oh my God, what did Rambo do?"

I'm not sure who asks that question, but it's one I have too. "Yesss..." I giggle as I take a drink.

"Y'all Rambo is used to us; he sat back there and slept. The entire time I was riding my husband," she laughs.

"How exciting was it?" Karsyn leans on her elbow.

"Legit one of the best times I've ever had. If you all can convince your men to go at it in a police cruiser, it's so worth it."

"Well first some of us have to get police boyfriends," Alisa reminds.

"I'm sure someone else besides Sully will move here soon." Ruby holds her glass up.

"Yes, let's toast on that." Alisa puts her glass up to everyone else's.

HOURS later we're closing the place down.

"We shouldn't drive home." Ruby giggles as she leans into me. "You think someone we know will come pick us up?"

I laugh along with her. "Hopefully Sully won't mind."

"Oh, I know my husband won't mind," Ruby snorts.

We're all standing outside the restaurant when numerous Laurel Springs PD cars pull up. Stella puts her arm on my shoulder. "We didn't even call them yet."

Sully and Ransom get out next to each other. "Y'all didn't have to." Sully grins, shaking his head as he looks at me. "Management placed a call to dispatch, asking us to come get the loud ladies closing the place down."

"Hector!" I yell at the manager. "How dare you rat us out?"

"I gotta go home," he argues. "I didn't feel safe knowing you all didn't have a ride."

"We gave you a great tip."

"And I'm thankful, but I won't have you ladies getting hurt on my watch."

"Thank you, Hector." Sully puts his arm around my waist. "We appreciate you, even if they don't."

"Traitor," I hiss to Hector.

"You'll still be back in here three weeks from now. I'm not worried."

"He's got your number." Nick goes over to retrieve his wife. "C'mon, let's get y'all home."

Little by little, the guys separate us into groups that they can take along their route. But we keep saying goodbye to each other, until a few of us are put in the back of the patrol cars.

"I can't believe you put me in the back of a patrol car, Caleb!" Ruby yells at her husband.

"You're lucky I don't take you in for being drunk in public."

"I'd like to see you try."

He laughs. "I'll see y'all later."

"C'mon, Counselor, let's get you home."

Trusting this man is the easiest thing I've ever done. Putting my hand in his, I grasp our fingers together. "Let's go."

CHAPTER 22
SULLIVAN

"DOMESTIC AT THIRTY-FIVE SIXTEEN LAUREL COURT."

I groan when dispatch comes over the radio with the address. Third time in the past month we've been called to this place.

"Neighbors are calling saying white male with no shirt on and a pair of jeans is beating a white woman in the front yard of the home. They've tried to intervene, but he's got a knife."

Immediately my adrenaline surges. The man at this home has been escalating, and I'm honestly surprised it's taken him this long.

"Show me as responding," I radio in.

"Me too." Nick's voice on the other end gives me a glimmer of hope. We're both big guys and possibly together we can take him down.

Flipping on my lights and sirens, I press the pedal on my Charger, feeling it respond underneath me. It doesn't have the same loud motor my Mustang does, but it has a lot of get up and go. While a huge part of me wants to race through the streets going as fast as I can, another part knows I have to be as safe as possible.

But what if I get there too late?

What if I don't get there at all?

These are the questions always tumbling through my mind when we have calls like this.

"Get the hell outta the way." I get in behind a truck, who must be out for a nice evening drive, because he's going all of thirty miles an hour, and can't seem to move out of my lane.

When I finally pass it, I glance over, giving a side-eye, only to see Mr. Honeycutt. He turned ninety-five last week. What the fuck is he still doing driving? I make a mental note to check on his license, before speeding up, hoping to get to my destination as soon as possible.

Rounding a curve, I spot Laurel Court. I've been here enough times since I came to town, I could get here in my damn sleep.

Fucking finally.

Flipping my eyes to my rearview, I see Nick in behind me.

Thank God I won't be dealing with this call on my own. We pull up right beside one another, getting out at almost the exact same time. There's a crowd gathered, and I'm almost scared to see what they're looking at.

Frank Gentry beating the holy hell out of his wife. She's curled up in a ball, her arms around her head trying to deflect the blows.

"Frank, get your hands up!"

Nick yells, pulling for his gun, squaring it on the man in front of us.

"Fuck you!" he fires back.

"I will tase you." I grab my taser out of its holster. "Get back from her now."

"Good luck, cocksucker," he spits in my direction.

I don't even think about it; I deploy the taser, watching as he drops to the ground. Nick and I are on him immediately, getting his hands behind his back. "I've got him." Nick hauls him off the ground, making sure not to do it easily. Neither one of us have any love for men who use their fists on their wives. "You get her."

As I rush off to check on Montana Gentry, I hear Nick reading her husband his rights.

"Montana." I drop to my knees, not knowing where to touch her, there's so much blood. "Let me know you're still alive," I beg her.

Reaching into my back pocket, I grab out a pair of rubber gloves, before keying the mic.

"Dispatch, make sure we have EMTs in route."

"They should be there ASAP."

ASAP isn't soon enough. Pulling the rubber gloves on, I do my best to perform a cursory examination. She moans pitifully when I check to see if he hurt her with a weapon.

"Did he have anything?" I ask softly, feeling for broken bones.

"Just his fists," she breathes out, shallow with a gurgling sound in the back of her throat.

The sound makes me sick, makes me wish I could change her life. Help her live one that she deserves. No one deserves what she's gotten.

"This isn't gonna stop, we can get you help," I start my spiel. The one I've given her every time we've come to their house. There isn't much hope she'll accept help, since she hasn't accepted it any of the other times I've offered. I still do it though, not because I have to, but because I want to. "You don't have to be his punching bag. You don't deserve this. Say the word and we'll charge him."

Her eyes, bloodshot and moist look up at me. She nods. It's almost imperceptible, so I have to ask. "You wanna us to charge him?"

Her busted lip makes talking difficult, but she pushes out a *yes*.

As the paramedics come to take over what I'm doing, there's a feeling in my gut. It's one I've never had so strongly before, and I know I'm doing the right thing when I jog to my patrol car and pull my phone from the console. I need her here. She needs her.

This number I know like the back of my hand now.

Waiting for it to be answered is more patience than have, but I manage. When I hear her voice, I croak out why I've called.

"Counselor, I need you..."

Shelby

I'M scared to death as I race to where Sullivan told me he was. Even I recognize the address.

Scared for Sullivan.

Scared for Montana.

And scared for myself.

My hands shake as I grip my steering wheel, the flashers hopefully letting other drivers know to get out of my way. Honking my horn at slower cars, I try and keep myself from letting the tears fall, but they're there.

Sullivan is hurting, which means I'm hurting too.

Within minutes I'm pulling up in front of the address. My tires screech as I come to a stop. I don't even turn it off before bailing out and running up to Sullivan.

"What happened?" I question as I get there, noticing a few more cops around and seeing the blood on Sullivan's uniform.

He points to me. "You need to come here."

I trip over my feet as I struggle to keep up with his long legs. He brings me to the back of an ambulance, where I see Cutter taking care of a woman. "Is this Montana?"

"It is." He gets up in the ambulance, bringing me with him. "Montana," he says to get her attention. "This is Shelby. Let her represent you, he's going to claim you beat him too," he whispers.

"Are you fuckin' kidding me?" I give him a glare.

"No, I'm not. He's already spoken to Nick. I need the two of you to get ahead of this."

Quickly I glance at Montana. "Okay, quick. I know most of your story because of Mrs. Haley, but I'm her attorney not yours. Do you have any money on you right now?"

She pulls a quarter out of her jeans pocket. "This is it."

"Right." I put it in mine. "I'm your attorney, and we'll have no comment when the officers come talk to you. There's no way he's going to turn this around. Do not speak to them, no matter how much you or I trust them, without me."

She nods. "We need to get you to the hospital and checked out. Right now you're my main concern. Cutter, can you get us there?"

"Yup, me and Devante will make sure you get there with no issue. She needs to have a few scans. She was hit in the head. Do you want to ride with us, or follow?"

I glance at Sully. "My car?"

"I'll make sure it gets home if you want to ride with her."

This man is the best one I've ever known. Lucky doesn't even begin to describe how I feel at this moment.

"Yeah, I would love to."

He leans down, kissing me softly before he exits the ambulance. Cutter follows, giving her and I some time on our own. I have to ask her the hard questions. Ones no woman wants to ask another.

"How many times has he done this to you, Montana?"

Her lip is busted and bleeding as she answers. Her words are slightly garbled as she speaks. It takes me a few minutes to understand what she's saying. "More times than I care to admit."

Reaching over, I grab a wet nap, helping her to blot at the blood, trying not to hurt her. I'm scared to touch her, there doesn't seem to be any part on her body that's not bruised and bloody. "When did it start?"

Tears build in her eyes. She tucks her lip, doubled in size into her mouth. "A month into our relationship. I burned the pizza," she whispers. "And he never let me forget it. It was a frozen one," she sobs. "Not even one we'd spent time making together. The oven in my apartment wasn't that great, and I usually ended up burning at least one thing a week. Just so happened this day, it was that pizza."

"I'm so sorry," I whisper, not imagining how this must be for her.

"I am too," she whispers back.

On impulse I reach out to grab her hand, wanting her to know she's not alone.

CHAPTER 23
SHELBY

"ARE YOU OKAY?" I ask Sully as we meet each other in the breezeway between our apartments.

"No, I hated letting you leave with her, knowing I wouldn't be there to make sure the two of you were safe from that fucker."

"I'm good, I promise."

His hands go immediately to my hair, burrowing deep. Before I can say anything, his mouth claims mine. This is different than any of the other kisses we've shared.

The hunger.

The possession.

It's everything I've always wanted and never had. He towers over me, encapsulating my body with his. Our fingers fight against each other, and I have no idea where he's taking us until Sullivan opens a door, and I know by the clean spicy scent we're in his apartment. He backs me up far enough until we get to his bedroom.

Instead of the passionate coming together we usually

have, this is slow. The setting sun shining through the window, bathing us in the glow of the afternoon.

Pulling back, I try to figure out how to get him out of his uniform. "Help me," I beg, my fingers failing in frustration.

"Give me a minute, I need to store my gear."

Sixty seconds is much too long, but I release him from my grip, having a seat on his bed while I watch him from across the room. Our eyes meet one another, his gaze traveling over my body mine taking in everything that keeps him alive while he's away from me. First he removes the gun from the holster, checks the chamber, and puts it in a safe I hadn't noticed before. The gun belt is next, draped over the chair beside his bed. Then he's dealing with the buttons of his uniform shirt.

"Come here." His low, sexy voice beckons me as he pulls the tails from his pants.

As quickly as I can, I'm up and over to where he stands. There's a bullet-proof vest covering his chest. "How do I get this off?"

"It's Velcro," he answers, grasping the back of my neck to pull me in to steal a kiss.

Trembling fingers find the closures, pulling on them and then lifting it up and over his head, causing us to break apart. He breathes deeply.

"You sound like you just took your bra off at the end of the day," I giggle, burying my face in the indent of his collar bone.

"I suppose it feels that way." He laughs along with me.

Underneath he wears a shirt and it's my pleasure to grip it in my fingers, yanking it over his head. He tries to pull my mouth back to him, but I resist, gazing up under my lashes.

"You've explored my body many times, Sully. It's my turn now."

Moving him around, I push him back against the bed, smirking when he bounces slightly. I'm wearing a dress today and it takes a small flick of my wrist at the back to have it in a pool at my feet. Black bra and panties are what I wore today, and had I known I'd be getting naked with Sullivan, I couldn't have picked anything better.

Before he can prop himself up on his elbows, I straddle his hips, putting my hands on his chest. I love the way he has a slight smattering of hair. So many men who have a body like his shave their chests. Mine though? He doesn't.

Leaning down I kiss from the first ab muscle at the top of his belly to his throat. Nipping, licking, and sucking as I make my way to his lips. He groans in satisfaction when we meet in a melding of passion. His fingers tangle in my hair adjusting me to his liking, although I'm on top. The other hand travels down my body, snaking under the lace of my panties.

"Sully," I moan as his fingers dip into my body from behind.

"You like that?" He smiles against my mouth.

"Yes! God yes!"

It's all he needs to flip me over, ripping the edges of my bra down so his lips can contour themselves to my left nipple. His right hand doesn't stop from where it's thumbing against my clit, pressing two fingers into my pussy.

I'm riding his fingers, seeking out his hard cock. It's jutting against me. Ripping his teeth from my peaked breasts, I force his eyes to meet mine. "I want you."

"We should have the talk." He presses himself up on his hands, hovering over me.

"The talk?"

"Birth control, Counselor. What do I need to do for you?"

God this man. He's not asking what I can do for him, but what he can do for me.

"I'm on the pill. I trust you if you feel the same as me."

He's up on his feet, stripping his uniform pants and underwear down. I have no idea where or how his shoes are taken off, all I know is when I move to unhook my bra and slip off panties his guttural voice stops me.

"Leave them on, Shelby."

Dark eyes run up and down my body as I lay on his bed, waiting for him to come to me. Running a finger up my arm, I play with the strap, pulling it slightly off. "What are you waiting on, officer?"

In a flash his body is covering mine. My hand goes between us grabbing his length, sighing excitedly when it kicks against my grip.

"I've been thinking about this for too long, Shelby. I wanna make it good for you."

"It will be." I guide him to my entrance, pulling the lace to the side. "If you knew how many times I touched myself thinking about you, you wouldn't have kept me waiting this long."

He growls as he eases into me. My fingers grip his shoulders, urging him on. "Fuck, Shelby." He buries his face in my neck. "You fit me like a goddamn glove."

"I was made for you," I gasp, moving my hands up to his hair, tugging tightly, pressing him further into my skin. "Don't take it easy on me, Sullivan. Give me everything."

He rises on his knees, spreading my thighs further apart, as he plunges and withdraws. If I could, I would clasp my legs around his waist and hold him tightly, but I'm spread too far apart by his legs, and the thumb he's managed to sneak between us again.

"Oh God," he grunts as he picks up the pace, causing the headboard to beat a steady rhythm against the wall. "Oh God, oh God, oh God," he sputters as his movements come to a crescendo.

I'm crazed as I do my best to keep up with him. Right as he goes still, caught in a strong thrust, he presses me over the edge. Together we come in an upheaval of bodies.

"Damn, Sully," I laugh slightly as I turn into his chest.

"I think you killed me," he accuses, his chest heaving.

Pressing up onto my shoulder, I give him a grin. "Maybe you should arrest me."

CHAPTER 24
SULLLIVAN

"DISPATCH, I'M TAKING LUNCH," I radio in as I pull up to The Café. It's been a long shift and I'm fucking starving. Rain moved in overnight, and it hasn't stopped in the last few hours.

"Gotcha, Sully."

Parking farther down than I'd like to, I get out, sprinting to the entrance, doing my best to stay dry. When I get under the awning, I slow my roll, shaking the water off my rain coat. Looking around to find an empty seat, I see the woman of my dreams at a booth by herself. Shelby's got her laptop to the side, a plate of food in front of her, and she's so focused on it, she hasn't noticed me. A spring in my step, I walk up to her table.

"Is this seat taken?"

Her gaze flies over to me, a smile spreading across her face. It's intimate, reminding me of the night we had, less than twenty-four hours ago. My thighs are still burning from the energy I expended making love to her.

"Hey," she whispers, biting her bottom lip, her eyes moving up and down my body.

"Hey," I answer back, giving her a smile of my own.

She scoots over, closing her laptop. "It's yours."

It's all the invitation I need to slide in next to her, draping my arm along the back of the seat. She turns into me, kissing my jawline. It's my favorite thing she does.

"You smell good."

"Rain and you." I lower my voice so only the two of us can hear.

Those green eyes of her soften. The mask she slides in front of everyone else as the strong woman she is drops for me. I'm lucky to see who she really is, and I'm beginning to understand how much she trusts me. It's enough to bring me to my knees.

"Sullivan, what can I get for ya?" Leigh asks as she walks up to our table.

"Wish I could say the biggest burger you've got, but Ransom and I are cutting right now. Grilled chicken and a whole plate of vegetables. Big, huge glass of water."

She laughs. "I've heard that same tone from my son."

"Why are you and Ransom cutting?" Shelby asks after she leaves.

"SWAT games in two months."

"You got something to prove?"

"We're up against Calvert City and Paradise Lost. My brother is on the PL SWAT team. You could say that. I tried out three times and was never accepted. I'd like to wipe the floor with them."

She puts her head on my shoulder. "You and your brother aren't close, are you? You don't talk about him much."

For most women, I don't ever want to talk about this, but with Shelby, I want her to know everything about me. "He and I were close until we both went for the police force. My dad, as good a dad as he is, pitted us against one another. Braylon was always his favorite."

"I'm sorry." She reaches over grabbing my chin. "I'd choose you."

My chest tightens. "You wouldn't be the first woman not to."

I didn't mean to say those words. This wasn't the time I wanted to bring it up, but another part of me thinks maybe I needed to get it out.

"Sullivan, what do you mean?"

"The woman I was kind of seeing at home, Candice. I worked hard to get her trust. We went round and round with each other for almost a year." I swallow, before I lick my lips. "She'd had a rough time, and I was okay with it, I was willing to work for her. We had a couple of dates, and I was ready to go all in. I took lunch one night and swung by her house. Only to find my brother there. It was obvious they were together. After that, I knew I had to make some changes. One of those changes was following Ro here."

"Well, I'm glad." She reaches up to caress my cheek. "If you hadn't come with her, I don't know that I would have met you."

I give her a smile. "I think we would have, Counselor. Something tells me we would have met, no matter what." Reaching over, I grab her hand, entwining my fingers with hers. "This is strong, and if it's this strong, it would've happened. Maybe not right now, but I believe it would've come back around to the two of us."

"Sully, you're not second best for me." She leans in, kissing me softly. "You're like the one and only."

"You're my one and only too."

"I hate to break this up." Leigh comes over to the table. "But your food is hot, and I wanted to make sure you got it that way."

"No problem." Shelby pulls away from me. "He needs a good meal to keep his mind on his work."

My stomach growls loudly as I smell the food in front of me. "How has your day gone?"

"Good," she answers. "I got a few new cases to work on, which has been nice. For a while there, I was starting to worry I'd made the wrong decision to come practice law here."

"As you said, we're both here for reasons that go beyond our control."

She giggles. "That's true." Reaching in, she grabs her burger, taking another bite. "I guess Mrs. Haley told her friends about me doing her will. I've got thirteen scheduled over the next few weeks."

"Babe, that's great!"

"I'll be able to keep the lights on, and then some." She winks.

Leaning in, I steal a kiss. "I have a question."

"I might have an answer."

"Menace is having everyone over for a dinner at his house as a get to know you type of thing for the LSERT. I'm not sure you heard about it."

"I got the email today. I hope he's got enough room."

"Same," I laugh. "I was wondering if you want to come with me?"

"Like a date?"

"Like a date, and it would be letting everyone know we're together."

She snorts. "I'm pretty sure everyone knows we're together."

"They may, but I'd love to have you there on my arm."

"Then I'd love to be there on your arm." She glances at her phone. "You can't have much longer on your lunch, you better get busy."

Looking at my watch, I see she's right. "I do need to hurry."

"Don't let me stop you."

Knowing I want to talk to her more than I want to eat, I settle with asking her a question. "What else do you have going on today?"

She takes one more fry before she pushes her plate away. "I'm going over a vendor contract for Eden, Mason's got a few contracts for LSERT stuff he wants me to take a look at, and I'm doing my end-of-month accounting. It's all very exciting stuff."

"Sounds like it." I play along with her.

"What do you plan on doing today?" she asks after I take my last bite of vegetables.

"Pray the rest of this shift goes by quickly. I've already worked a wreck and had to pull over a douchebag in a Porsche doing eighty in a thirty-five."

"A Porsche? Awful nice car for around here."

A shit-eating grin flashes across my face. "Some big shot attorney trying to get to Birmingham."

She laughs. "It would be an attorney."

"Right? Exactly my thoughts."

She pushes against my shoulder. "Stop being such an ass."

"That's not what you called me last night."

She rolls her eyes. "Just because you were awesome last night doesn't mean you'll always be awesome."

"Hurt my pride, Counselor."

"I don't think anything can hurt your pride. You have plenty."

Leigh walks by, and I put up my hand. "Bring us the check?"

"You know I don't charge y'all." She waves off.

"And you know we hate that." I pull out cash from my wallet and walk over to drop it in the tip jar. "Have a good one, Leigh." I wave at her as I go back to the table to get Shelby.

"You too." She waves bye to us.

"Walk you back to your office?" I hold my arm out to Shelby.

She grins. "Look at you being a gentleman."

"I'm always a gentleman."

She waits until we get out of The Café. "You weren't last night."

My arm goes around her waist, my mouth next to her ear. "And you wouldn't have it any other way."

"Truth," she giggles. "I gotta get back to work." She turns to face me as we stop in front of her office.

"I do too, but I hope to see you tonight?"

"We'll see if I have time for you."

I throw my head back, laughing at her. Slowly, I put my arms around her waist, pulling her in close. "Make time for me?"

She tips her head up, smirking. "I'll always make time for you."

CHAPTER 25
SHELBY

THE ALARM on my phone goes off, letting me know it's time to end this work day.

SULLY: Are we gonna hang out tonight?
COUNSELOR: Definitely, but I haven't left yet. I'm fixing to, though. Keep in mind I need to go by the hospital to see Montana. I'll be home right after. Do you want to come to my place, or me to yours?"
SULLY: You make the decision.
COUNSELOR: I'll see ya in a little while.
SULLY: Be safe, Counselor.

The way he always tries to make sure I'm okay goes straight to my heart. There's been no one in my life that's ever cared about my safety the way he does. If I had someone like that in Houston, I probably wouldn't be in Laurel Springs right now. Just goes to show, things happen how they're supposed to.

It takes a few minutes for me to make sure the lights are

turned off and I've packed my laptop. I do one more cursory glance around the office before I go to the alarm, setting it quickly and exiting the building. At one point I'd thought I wouldn't need the alarm, but now with Montana and Frank, I'm glad I sprung for it.

The days are getting longer, evidenced by the sun still in the sky as I leave. It wasn't but a few weeks ago it was dark when I left the office. Like everyone else, I enjoy the vitamin D.

Getting into my car, I open the sunroof and put down the back windows. Sunglasses pop over my eyes and I inhale deeply. Summer is close; the smell washes over me, giving me hope that everything is gonna be okay. Backing out of my spot, I slowly pass The Café, where I see Frank eyeing me from inside.

I look back at him, not cowering, like I'm sure he would want me to. If he wants a fight. I can bring one, and he won't be able to run over me as easily as he did Montana.

"HEY, GIRL, WHAT ARE YOU DOIN' here?" I hear as I walk into the Laurel Springs Medical Center. "You're okay, aren't you?"

"Hey, Alisa," I greet one of the newest members of our group. "I'm here to see a patient, actually."

"Do you know where they are? I can help you."

Last night, I left Montana before she'd been admitted. "I'm not sure what floor she's on. I'd appreciate any help I can get."

"Follow me."

"It was good hanging out with you the other night." I tag along behind her, securing my purse on my shoulder.

She turns around, giving me a huge smile. "Agreed, I haven't met a ton of people since I moved here, so it was nice. Thanks for allowing me to be a part of the group."

"Girl, I'm new too," I laugh. "Not as new as you, but it's been a little over a year. The way people accept you in this community is something I've never been used to before."

"Yeah, I'm from Florida and I don't even think I had a group of friends like this, there."

"I know exactly what you mean. I'm from Houston, and I probably had one or two really good friends, but in the end they weren't who I thought they were."

"Isn't that always the way it goes?"

We come to an admit desk. "Who is your friend you're coming to find?"

"Montana Gentry. I'm her attorney."

"Can you show me your ID, she has a list of people allowed to see her."

The extra security makes me feel good. Reaching into my purse, I grab my wallet, opening it and flashing my identification. "You're on the list."

"I'll take you to where she is." Alisa waves me to follow her.

"How do you like working here?" I ask her as we get on the elevator and go up to the fourth floor.

"It took some getting used to. It isn't nearly as busy here as it was there. Every shift I would go home exhausted. After these shifts I most of the time go for a workout."

"It's definitely a much slower pace than I was used to, too. I'm starting to like it though."

"Me too." Alisa smiles as the elevator comes to a stop.

I follow her down the hallway, halting in front of a closed door.

"I'm going to be straight with you," she says as she turns around to face me. "I took care of her when she was assigned a room last night. She looks rough."

"I know, I rode with her in the back of the ambulance."

"They typically look worse in the days that follow."

"I understand," I say but my heart is already breaking for what I know I'm going to see when she opens the door.

"Hey, Montana." Alisa's voice is happy and upbeat. "You've got someone here to see you. Is there anything I can get you while I'm here?"

"Maybe some more ice chips."

"That's easy. Let me go get those for you."

She leaves and we're alone for the first time since the back of the ambulance. "How are you doing?" I ask her as I have a seat across from her.

"Hurting some this afternoon." She adjusts in the bed.

I allow myself to look at her. Really look at her. Her face is purple and red, bruised to hell and back. Her lips are split and doubled in size. The left cheek is stitched up over the bone.

"I'm so sorry this happened to you."

She shrugs. "I've learned you have to change your own future. For so long, I've just let my life continue on with status quo. For the last few weeks I've been thinking about it. What I should be doing, and it's definitely not this. If I want respect from a man, I have to learn to respect myself. I can't keep making excuses for why I put up with being treated this way. It's time for me to get what I deserve."

"I totally agree with you. Do you have a safe place where

you can go when you get out of here? If you don't, I'll make sure you're safe."

She nods, licking her dry lips as Alisa comes back in.

"Here's your ice chips, is there anything else I can get you? It's another hour until your next pain medication dose."

"No, I'm good."

Alisa gives a smile before leaving.

"Do I need to make arrangements for you to go somewhere safe when you get out of here?"

She looks down at her hands clasped in her lap. "I don't have any of my own money. It's all his."

I want badly to tell her what Mrs. Haley has put into her will, but I'm bound by confidentiality. "I'll make sure you have a place to go, Montana, you have nothing to worry about."

There's a drop to her shoulders, tears pooling in her eyes. "I've done nothing but worry for the last few years. What's going to happen with the case against him?"

"He's tried to push it off on you, but there were multiple eye-witnesses. We're waiting for a warrant to be issued, but it will be. Trust me."

"I've lost trust in a lot of people, Shelby."

"I know you have, but I promise you can trust me."

She's hesitant, but finally she nods before whispering. "I know I can."

AFTER LEAVING MONTANA'S ROOM, I know there's one place I have to go. A couple of days ago, I was notified that Mrs. Haley was brought in for palliative care, and if there's one thing I want to give her before she goes, it's peace.

Walking to the nurse's station, I see Stella. "Hey." I wave at her, exhausted, but on a mission.

"Hey, I heard you were with Montana when she was brought in," Stella puts her hands on her hips. "How's she doing?"

"Best as can be expected. Speaking of though, can you tell me what room Mrs. Haley's in? I'm her attorney."

Stella smiles sadly. "I'm going down there right now to administer some more medication, actually. Wanna follow me?"

"Definitely." I fall in line behind her. "Is she lucid?"

"Before we give her medicine, yes." Stella looks over at me. "Do you want me to hold off a few minutes."

"Will it be unbearable for her?"

"I honestly think not knowing if Montana is safe or not is more unbearable than the pain she's feeling right now."

The two of us walk in. I almost don't recognize the woman who was in my office not long ago. She's gone downhill quickly. "Hey, Mrs. Haley."

"Shelby?"

"Yeah." I reach out to grab her hand. "It's me."

"Is something wrong?"

"I just wanted to let you know, Frank was arrested tonight. Montana is safe, and I'll make sure she stays that way." Reaching down, I move her gray hair out of her face. "I've got her now."

"Thank you," she breathes out. "I'm so tired."

"I know you are."

She closes her eyes, looking ghostly against the sheets.

"Mrs. Haley, are you ready for your medicine?" Stella asks.

"Yes." Her voice is small, almost withering away.

Knowing she doesn't have much time left, I lean in. "It was a pleasure to meet you, Mrs. Haley."

She grasps my hand in hers. "You too, Shelby. You're going to do great things."

And as I leave, I let the tears fall for this family who've dealt with so much adversity in their lives. At least this is one thing I could make right for them.

"HOW WAS MONTANA?" Sully asks as he sits on the other end of the couch away from me, handing a bowl of chocolate ice cream to me.

"I'm eating ice cream for dinner. What does that tell you?"

He reaches out with his foot, hitting mine. "I'm eating ice cream with you. Must mean my day was bad too."

"Or that you're a good boyfriend who feels my pain." I grin. "She's doing okay. Scared, beat to hell, and wondering what's going to happen with the rest of her life. I mean who wouldn't. He controls the purse strings, she doesn't work." I take a huge bite of the ice cream. "It's one of the reasons I decided to start my own practice when I came here. I wanted to make sure I could support myself."

He's quiet as he asks. "Is there a particular reason for that?"

"Let's just say I put my trust in people I never should have in Houston. I got caught up in a case, which had nothing to do with me, but it put me in a bad situation. There was an investigation and I lost everything I've always worked for. When I came to Laurel Springs, it was with five hundred bucks in my bank account and no client list. Since then I've never given my future up to anyone other than myself."

"You know you can trust me with your future, right?"

I put my spoon in the bowl, sitting it down on the coffee table. "I *want* to believe that, Sully. I do."

He closes the space between us, gathering me up in his arms. "I'll prove it to you." He drops a kiss on my forehead. "I know it's gonna take more than my word."

I hook my hands in the curve of his biceps, pulling him even closer. "I wish I could take your word."

"I get it." He puts his forehead to mine. "Actions speak louder, and I've always been a man of action."

CHAPTER 26
SHELBY

"THANKS FOR MEETING ME," Kels says as I slide in, holding my coffee.

"You didn't have to ask me twice. I love the cinnamon rolls here."

A Whole Latte Love has become one of our favorite places to meet.

"Me too." She takes a drink of her frappé. "I asked to have mine heated up."

I giggle. "Yes, that's why I didn't bring it to the table with me."

"It was good seeing you at girls night out."

This isn't why she's invited me here. I've known her long enough to know she's beating around the bush. One thing I've learned is to let people come to me. In their own time, they'll tell you what they want.

"I can see why our cinnamon rolls are taking a few minutes," Kelsea grins, nodding her head toward the cash register.

Trying not to be obvious, I slowly turn. "Oh my God," I hiss as I see Devante and Eden talking to one another.

They're obviously flirting, if I'm going by the grin on her face and the way he's leaning up against the counter.

"Get you some," Kelsea whisper-hisses, which causes me to snort.

Luckily they're so involved with one another, they don't even pay attention to us. "Wonder what they're saying?" I move around so that I can see them from where we're sitting.

"I'm sure he's like 'Baby, wanna come ride in the back of my ambulance?'"

I hide my lips behind my hand, dropping my voice to imitate a man's. "We got a gurney, and oxygen if you need it. 'Cause girl, I'm gonna steal your breath."

"Stop," she giggles.

This time Eden looks over at us, and we do our best to act like we've not been watching their exchange. Somehow I don't think she believes us, but we're saved as Cutter rushes in.

"D, we gotta go!"

Before we know it, they rush out and the three of us are left in the shop. We watch as Eden finishes heating up our cinnamon rolls. When she brings them over, Kels gives her a sly grin.

"So, how's Devante?"

Eden playfully glares at us. "You two weren't as discreet as you thought you were."

"Neither were the two of you." I give her a look.

"It's not even a thing," she protests.

"We never said it was." Kels takes a sip of her frappé. "We just wanted our cinnamon rolls."

I laugh. "No, we want the scoop. What's going on with you and the EMT hottie?"

"We haven't gone on a date or anything yet, but you're right, he's super-hot. He has the best smile, and he always smells amazing."

"Oh yeah, girl. You got it bad."

"So do you." She gives me my cinnamon roll.

"I don't deny how bad I have it for Sullivan."

"Well, I'd love to sit here and chat, but I have to start getting product ready for tomorrow. I'll be in the back. Just yell if you need anything, ladies."

I wait for her to disappear into the back, before I turn to face Kelsea. "Why'd you wanna meet me today, Kelsea? I got the feeling from you text that there's something you want to talk about?"

She takes a bite of her pastry. "Nick and I've been talking about the future."

The way she says the words, I believe she's speaking about more than what they're going to have done before the end of the year. "And what can I do to help you with your future?"

"Both of us have been thinking about where the kids would be if either of us got hurt in the line of duty, or just driving down to Birmingham for a night out. Where would they go in the immediate moments after? Who would take them? If we don't have something in writing, what could happen? We've been having long discussions about this."

Reaching down, I take out my yellow legal pad I always carry with me. It's got a pen attached to it. "Do you and Nick know who you want to take care of your children? Have you spoken with the people you trust? It's always good to give them a heads up."

She plays with her cup. "We spoke with Caleb and Ruby. They're willing to take on our kids, unless D is of age. Darren has agreed if he's of age, he wants to take care of his sister."

"Are you sure?" I stop writing for a second. "It's a lot of responsibility."

"He's been responsible for as long as we've known him."

Somehow I believe that. "Okay, so what about your assets? We need to figure out what those are to give your children the best care."

"Both of us have life insurance policies on each other through our jobs, and we've paid to increase those amounts. I have a million dollars on Nick and he has eight hundred and fifty thousand on me."

"What about your debts? Those will be probated with the will. Anything we need to know about?"

"We're debt-free except for the house. We have a five-year plan to pay it off. If something happens to us, our life insurance should more than take care of it. We already have college accounts for the kids."

I blink quickly. "The two of you are incredibly fiscally responsible."

"It's important to Nick and that makes it important to me. Growing up the way he did, money is a safety net for him."

"Completely understandable." I make another note. "Is there anyone else you'd like to put in, as a backup?"

"I can change it later, right?"

"Of course. As things happen in life and there are changes, we can update. There will always be a copy available at my office, and I'll file a copy with the courts. Because of the job Nick does, they also request it be placed in their files as the police department. I'll make sure all this is taken care of."

She breathes a sigh of relief. "Thank you, Shelby. Can you please send me a bill?"

"A bill? This was a couple of friends meeting for coffee."

"No, it wasn't. I just couldn't make an appointment. I know it seems dumb, but it almost felt as if I was tempting fate. Like if I made the appointment to finalize a will, Nick would be killed on his way home."

"It's not dumb. Trust me, I get it."

She takes a sip of her coffee and eyes me over the cup. Lifting an eyebrow, she smirks before speaking. "Sullivan, huh? You're deep, aren't you, Shelby?"

"I am, so deep that I'm going to Mason's cookout tomorrow afternoon."

She throws her head back laughing. "Welcome to the family, girl."

CHAPTER 27
SULLIVAN

"ARE you sure there's nothing I can bring?" Shelby asks me for the third time.

Reaching over, I grab hold of her hand, before bringing it up to my lips. "I'm positive. I asked Mason like you wanted me to, and he said to bring ourselves."

"Just checking."

"You've checked plenty of times, babe. There's no reason for you to worry about this. You know all of these people."

She rolls her eyes. "I do, but I know them in an LSERT capacity. Not in a friendly capacity."

"Oh, I think you and the girls are *very* friendly. Especially if you ask Hector," I laugh, avoiding her hand as she tries to smack me.

"You know what I mean."

"No, I don't. Everyone knows you, Shelby."

"But they don't me like this."

"Like what, babe? You've got to spell this out for me, because I ain't getting it."

"As your girlfriend. We're a couple now. Not just Shelby

or Sullivan. Now we're kind of Shelby *and* Sullivan. Shelivan if you will. We've made the jump," she says like I should know.

"We made the jump weeks ago."

"Not officially," she argues.

"Whatever," I laugh, reaching over as we come to a stop light. I rub her bottom lip with the pad of my thumb. "We've been official since Christmas when I first kissed these lips."

"You think so?"

"I know so."

She doesn't say anything as we pull up to the Harrison's house, even though I hear her intake of breath at the amount of cars, trucks, and SUVs lined along the curb. "You okay?"

"Yeah, it's just more people than I thought there would be."

"You see almost all these people at the LSERT meetings."

"But not their families too," she argues.

"They're going to love you," I encourage her. "You've done a lot for everyone here. You came and did the wills for anyone at the PD who wanted it. You work hard and you're a genuine person. They're going to adore you as much as I do." I lean forward, tilting my head down to her. She meets me halfway, our lips connecting in a less-than-chaste kiss for where we are, but I indulge her. I'll always indulge her. As I pull away, a horn honks behind us. Turning, I see Cutter and Ro. It's Cutter at the wheel though, waving like a goofy fucking idiot. Lifting my middle finger, I wave back at him.

"Sully," she giggles, burying her face in my chest.

"He and I have a love/hate relationship. Right now, I hate his ass."

"Stop." She gives me a look before turning around to get out of the car.

She and Ro greet each other. They're both still slightly shy with one another. I hope later they become as close as I am with the two of them. "How's it going?" I ask Cutter.

"It's been pretty damn busy." He stretches.

"I know, the warmer it gets, the worse it gets."

"I'm surprised all of you were able to get the day off," Shelby says as she comes around my Mustang to put her hand in mine.

"Calvert City is covering. We do the same for them a few times a year," Cutter explains.

The four of us walk to the back of Mason and Karina's house. We can hear the party already in full swing. There are kids in the pool, men manning the grill, and women putting out a spread of food. People wave to us as we come in, Caleb handing out beers.

"Welcome, welcome," he greets. "You'll find a shit ton of food, drinks, and kids." He grins.

"Should we go see if they need help?" Shelby asks gripping my hand tightly.

"The only thing you should do," - I put my arm around her shoulder, taking a drink of my beer – "is stay right here by my side."

It's amazing for me to see the group of people together like this. Even though my family is close, after what happened with Braylon, I started distancing myself. Whether I've wanted to admit it or not, I've missed this part of my life. Instead of making my family choose, I've pulled away.

I'VE GOT a plate balanced on my knee and a fork halfway to my mouth when Mason gets up in front of everyone.

"First of all I wanna thank everybody for coming by today. I know time off is special and you protect it. None of us get to spend enough time with our families. So I appreciate you giving me the afternoon. Because of your hard work, we've been given a grant by the state of Alabama. With the money we'll be able to get from the auction, along with this, we're going to do some big things. There will be a vote, though," - he tries to shut down the clapping and hooting that's coming from the group of us - "we'll decide as a group what we're going to get."

My chest swells with pride. I'm doing something here I wasn't in Paradise Lost. Something that makes a difference in the community.

A service that isn't connected to a family.

I've chosen to give my time, my expertise to a group of people who appreciate me.

This right here? It's the calling I've always wanted and never had. These are the friends and family I've chosen, and I'm damn glad I did.

Shelby

I JUMP when my phone rings. It's not very often my office phone gets a call, so my heart pounds as I reach for it. "Shelby Bruce's office."

"Shelby, hey it's Stella."

"Why are you calling my office phone?"

Immediately I'm worried. For her to call this number, something has to be wrong.

Her voice is low and full of apology. "It was in Mrs. Haley's information, to call you when she passed."

"Oh no!"

"Yeah, about an hour and a half ago. You have her final wishes?"

Sighing heavily, I dig into my filing cabinet to find the information she gave me about how she wanted the last of her wishes to go. Grabbing the file, I throw it on the desk. "I do, is there anything I need to come down there and take care of?"

"Just let me know which funeral home she wants to use and I'll call them for you."

"Thank you." I do my best to keep the tears out of my voice. I shouldn't be this emotional about a client. It's not good to get involved, but this woman touched a place inside my heart. "I'll take care of everything else."

"Okay, my thoughts are with you, Shelby."

"Thanks, Stella."

After I hang up the phone, I break down. Tears stream down my face, and I sob. For the love this woman had in her heart. For Montana, who doesn't know how she was loved by others.

For myself.

The last client I lost was a child I'd not been able to save. Just like I hadn't been able to save Mrs. Haley.

Fumbling with my cell phone, I dial a number that's become my lifeline. Sniffling, I speak when he answers. The same words he'd said to me.

"Sully, I need you."

"Shelby, what's wrong?"

"Mrs. Haley." I barely get the words out. "She died."

"Oh, Counselor, I'll be right there."

After I hang up, I collapse into myself. I don't expect him to be here quickly, but I hear the door open, along with Sullivan's worried voice.

"Shelby, are you okay?"

"No," I sob, getting up to throw my arms around him. "Can you just take me home?"

"Yeah, let me call in." He moves his chin over my shoulder, grabbing his radio to alert dispatch.

I'm not even sure what he says, but I let him hold me. I let him do what I haven't let anyone else do before. I trust him enough to make sure I break down safely. To let myself feel all the emotions and not worry about the ugly-cry. Not obsess over the wrecked voice, or the red eyes.

And Sullivan Baker? He doesn't disappoint when he tucks me into bed that night.

He slides in right next to me, putting my head against his chest, and allowing me to hold him tightly.

"She died by herself," I whisper to him. "She wouldn't allow Frank to be a part of her life, so she decided to be alone. Can you imagine? Dying alone?"

"No." He pushes my hair back from my forehead, stroking it tenderly.

I lean into the touch, wanting nothing more than to lose myself in the heat we normally have, but I can't do it tonight. Tonight I need the soft side of not only Sully, but myself.

"I always used to worry about it," I sniffle. "Ya know, since I moved here by myself. Like what if something happened to me? Who would know?"

"Well now you know you're never going to have to worry about that ever again."

CHAPTER 28
SHELBY

IT'S a quiet day and I'm slightly thinking about leaving early, especially after the day and night I had. Not even the joy of letting Montana know about her good fortune has been enough to soothe my soul about Mrs. Haley.

It's a beautiful afternoon, and I'd love to go for a walk. Reaching over for my phone, I debate on who I can ask to go with me. Scrolling through, I stop at Rowan's name. The two of us haven't done much on our own, and if I can see myself being in Sullivan's life, I need to be in hers too.

S: Are you busy this afternoon? I'm thinking of taking a walk.

R: Ohhh sounds good, what time? I get off at three. Want me to meet you at your office? I have workout clothes I can change into here.

S: Me too, I'll see you then.

Putting my phone over to the side with a smile on my face, I'm excited to be spending some more time with her.

She's the most important person in Sullivan's life, and I know if I want to be in his, I need to be in hers.

Sighing, I take a glance at the amount of paperwork in front of me. It's going to be a long morning until I'm able to take the much-needed walk. Opening my desk drawer, I grab out my wallet. It's the perfect day for an iced coffee.

There's a line out the door for The Café. Glancing at my watch, I see it's lunch time, and today is fried catfish as the special. I'm not a fish lover, but I've heard from literally everyone else in town how good it is.

I wave at Leigh as I pass by. "You don't need my money today."

She laughs. "If you want some coffee, it might be a wait. Eden's isn't as slammed."

"I'm gonna go see her."

When I walk into *A Whole Latte Love*, there's a few patrons and Eden's standing behind the counter. "I need an iced coffee, stat," I beg as I walk up to the register.

She grins, her brown eyes twinkling. "That after lunch drag hitting you hard?"

"It's more like I wanna play hooky."

"Doesn't it suck owning your own business? There's no way you can call in because there's no one else to do the job."

"Oh my God, you hit the nail right on the head. Sometimes I don't want to be responsible."

"Unfortunately the bills have to be paid though."

I sigh as she starts making my coffee. "Don't I understand it? Maybe one day we'll be rich enough to have our own staffs."

"That's the life." She sighs along with me. "Here's your coffee."

"Thanks." I grab a ten dollar bill out of my wallet, handing it to her.

"Your money is no good here, Shelby." She tries to push it back to me.

"No, you forget that as a fellow small business owner, I know we aren't ever going to have a staff if we keep giving our shit away for free."

She rolls her eyes. "Okay, but at least let me give you your change."

"I'll allow that." I hold out my hand, laughing as she makes a face. "If your mouth doesn't say it, your face will," I giggle.

"Unfortunately you're right about that."

Scooping up my change and coffee, I give her a wave. "See ya, I need to get back to work. Hopefully this will take me through my rut."

"See ya," she answers my wave with one of her own.

Exiting the coffee shop, I feel the sun on my face and I take a moment to tilt up into it. The winter was long and lonely, but the spring and summer months are definitely looking up. Maybe I can convince Sully to take me to Paradise Lost and show me around. Although I'm from the south, I've never been to the beach, and I've heard his hometown has one of the best in the world.

I'm so lost in my own thoughts I don't notice the car outside my office, and I don't pay attention to the man standing inside until we're face-to-face with one another.

Frank Gentry.

"Can I help you?" Somehow I manage to keep the fear out of my voice.

His eyes stare me down. Blue fire and a hatred I've never seen before. In Houston I defended victims against some of the cruelest of criminals, yet I've never seen eyes as cold as this man's.

"Yeah, you can tell me what the fuck you talked that old bitch into."

My head whips back as if he's reached out and slapped me. "Excuse me?"

"You know what I'm talking about. Her millions were going to be mine until you talked her into giving them to Montana."

"I can't discuss with you what your grandmother wanted for her final wishes. She's deceased and it doesn't negate attorney/client privilege. I have nothing to tell you, Frank. I'd appreciate it if you left."

He turns from me, his back rigid. My eyes stray to his hands which are clenched in fists at his side. I have a seat on my desk, discreetly pulling my phone closer to my body. This situation doesn't feel good to me and I want to make sure I have a way to call for help.

"Don't tell me to leave." He faces me quickly. "You're going to listen to me."

"No, I'm not. There's nothing for us to discuss."

"That's where you're wrong. We have a lot to discuss." He advances toward me.

As quickly as I can, I try to dial 911, but the phone is ripped out of my hand before I can finish.

"No, no we don't."

"Yes we do." He grabs hold of my shoulder. "I need that money!"

I fight against his grip. "It makes no difference what you need. Your grandmother signed a legally binding document. There's nothing you're going to be able to do to change it, Mr. Gentry."

"Don't placate me. Don't sit there and sanctimoniously call me Mr. Gentry," he says the words between clenched teeth.

"I'm asking you to think about what you're doing here, and leaving. You're already in enough trouble."

"No thanks to you, you stupid bitch!"

"You think calling me a bitch makes me hate you?" I scream back at him.

"It gets under your skin," he baits me.

"All it does is make you feel like a bigger man." I jerk my arm free of his grip, folding it over my chest.

"I'll show you what makes me feel like a bigger man." He pushes me back against the wall, raising his arm over my head.

Instinctively I twist away from him.

"Shelby! I know I'm early!"

I've never been so glad to hear Rowan's voice in my life. Frank drops my hand, releasing me from the wall.

I push as far away from him as I can. Rowan walks into my office, immediately stopping as she undoubtedly feels the tension in the room.

"Is everything okay here?"

"It's fine." He gives us both a smile as he exits the office.

"Is it?" she asks as she takes a look at me.

I'm shaking, running my hands through my hair. "It will be," I sigh. "I'm ready for that walk."

"Shelby, do you want me to call Sullivan?" she questions.

As much as I want her to, I can't lean on him like this. Whenever things go wrong, I can't call him and lay all my problems out to him. There are some things I need to take care of on my own.

"No, I got this. Let me go change."

Going into the bathroom, I close and lock the door. Not because I don't feel safe with Rowan, but because I need to that extra layer of security right now. That bastard coming into a place I've always felt comfortable in pisses me off. Slamming the lid down, I have a seat and let the tremors go through my body. Before I decide I'm not going to let him fuck up my day.

"I'M INVITING him to help me pick out a wedding dress," Ro says, slightly breathless as we stroll through downtown.

"Sullivan?" I try to keep the laughter out of my voice.

"Yeah," she chuckles. "He's my best friend."

"Which tells me more than anything about what a good guy he is."

"He is, he's a great guy. Which is why I've always wanted him to have the best there is. I have to tell you." She stops, looking at me. "I've never seen him as happy as he is with you."

"The same could be said for me."

"Are you going to tell him about what happened with Frank? You can't convince me something didn't happen with him."

I'm quiet as I wonder what I want to do.

I want to be a strong woman. One that Sullivan deserves.

"I haven't decided yet, but I'll do what I think is best."

CHAPTER 29
SHELBY

"FRANK WAS NOTIFIED yesterday by certified mail."

Montana gapes, her mouth wide open. "She gave all this money to me?"

"She did." I nod, watching as she looks at the will I wrote for Mrs. Haley. "She knew what kind of a situation you were in. It was her last wish for you to have this and to get away from him."

Tears trail down her cheeks. "She knew. This whole time?"

"From what I understand she did."

"He's going to be pissed." Her hands shake as she wipes at the tears. "Not only at me, but at you too."

"I can handle him." I shuffle around in my bag. "Here's your first check from the estate. I know you get out of the hospital in a couple of days. If you would like me to deposit this for you into an account we set up for you, I can do that. Then you can start trying to find a new place to live."

"How will I move there? I can't lift anything." She's still in shock, looking at me with amazement in her eyes.

"You let me take care of that. There are plenty of people around here willing to help you."

"I don't know how to thank you," she cries.

"Live a life you love, Montana. It's all I want."

"I can do it because of you." She reaches out, grabbing my hand.

AS I DRIVE AWAY from the hospital, I pick my phone up and call someone I don't call nearly enough. It rings about eight times and I'm about to give up when they answer.

"Shelby! It's been too long."

"Hey, Mom." I smile as I hear her voice. "I know, I've been busy trying to get everything set up here."

"I wish you had let me and your dad come help you."

It's what she always says. "I had to do this myself."

"No you didn't, but I know you're stubborn. How are things going?"

"I've met somebody." I grin as I whisper the secret I've been keeping too myself.

"You like him too, I can tell by the way your voice lowered, and there's a smile."

"I do, I love him," I admit for the first time to anyone, including myself.

"Then we can't wait to meet him. How is your practice doing?"

"Good, the case I just had was crazy..."

"YOU'RE QUIET TONIGHT," Sully says as we sit on my couch, eating the sushi he picked up on his way home.

"I had an interesting day."

He takes a bite, before sitting his plate down on the coffee table. "Does it have anything to do with the bruise on your arm?"

I put my plate down beside his. "I was hoping you didn't see that."

He turns to face me, hooking his thumb under my chin. "At this point, you should know I notice everything about you. I been waiting for you to come to me, but now I'm coming to you. Tell me what happened today."

"Frank came to see me."

His face turns red almost immediately. "That son of a bitch did this to you?"

"He was upset about losing the money to Montana."

"So he thinks it's okay to put his hands on you? I'm not okay with that. Why didn't you call me?"

Sighing, I run a hand through my hair. "Because I wanted to take care of this myself."

"This shit I take care of for you, Counselor. You don't deal with this yourself. You come to me." He's barely holding it together.

My heart swells as I hear the words coming out of his mouth. "Don't hurt him, please. I don't want you to get in trouble because of what he did to me."

"Oh I will hurt him within the limits of the law. No one touches someone I care about. You can't expect me to make exceptions for that. There are no exceptions when it comes to you."

Instead of saying anything, I smile, throwing my arms

around his waist, snuggling in close. "I know I'm safe with you, Sully."

"Always," he whispers. "You're always safe with me."

Sullivan

TWO DAYS **Later**

"Thank you for doing this." Shelby puts a cup of coffee in my hand. "I know you were on-shift late last night, and thank you for bringing your friends. I promise I'll grab some breakfast on our way over there."

"They're your friends too, babe," I remind her.

"But none of you have to do this."

"She needs help, and we help the members of the community."

"Don't lie." She stands on her tiptoes to kiss me on the cheek. "You kinda hope Frank shows up so you can arrest him."

"Can you fucking blame me? I'm still pissed he showed up at your office the way he did. I'd like to kick his ass, and I don't care how I do it. Whether it be him harassing you or his wife."

"Where do you want this?" I ask Montana as I carry in a bag she'd put into a storage unit a few months ago.

She's sitting on a couch in a safe apartment building, thanks to the money Mrs. Haley left her. And because of Shelby too. It's nice to see her basically holding court while the three of us carry boxes into this place. It's got a built-in security system, along with a doorman.

First building like this in Laurel Springs.

Not gonna lie, I'm thinking about trying to convince

Shelby we need to live here. When I'm not with her, I worry constantly for her safety."

"If you can just put it over there." Montana points to a clear spot on the ground. "I'll go through it all when I feel like it."

Dropping the box where she asked me to, I make another trip outside.

"This is the last one," Cutter says as he walks by me.

"That's it?"

"She didn't have much." Shelby keeps her voice low. "Most of what she's going to have will be new."

"Understandable. You wanna hang around and make sure she's okay before we leave?"

Her arms clasp tightly around my waist. Encompassing her, I pull her to my chest, slipping her head under my chin.

"You're the best man I've ever known, Sully, and I would love to stick around until she says it's okay."

Dipping down, I put drop a kiss to the top of her head. "You make me better."

She releases me, smiling widely. "Let me go in and check on her."

"I'll go with you."

Holding her hand we walk inside Montana's new apartment. Cutter and Rowan are unpacking boxes while she tells them where everything needs to go.

"Do you want us to do these?" Shelby asks as she points to a group of boxes we've put in the corner.

"No, those are personal things." She shakes her head. "Y'all have done enough."

"If you need anything, please don't hesitate to call us." I hand her a card with my cell number on it. "This building has one of the best security systems I've ever seen. You're going to be safe here, but if you need anything, we're only a phone call away."

"Thank you." She grasps my hand. "You don't know how much I appreciate this."

"Anything Shelby asks me for, I'm willing to do." I laugh as I put my arm around Shelby's neck.

"She's a lucky lady."

Glancing over at her, I feel the soft smile sliding across my face. "Nah, I'm a very lucky man."

CHAPTER 30
SULLIVAN

"DOMESTIC DISPUTE AT THE CAFÉ," dispatch advises, causing me to do a double-take when I hear the location.

"The Café?" I verify.

"Yes. Caller states two patrons are having a disagreement."

I can hear Leigh screaming on the call. "It's Montana and Frank Gentry. He's cornered her here."

Son of a bitch. "I'll be right there."

I'm driving a Charger today instead of my customary SUV. As it responds to the way my foot presses the gas, I kind of hope they let me have it for the long haul. Even though I started out halfway across the county, I'm in front of The Café within minutes.

There's a crowd, and I can see Frank standing very close to his wife.

"Frank, back away, or I'm going to have to take you in. You're aware there's an order of protection against you."

I don't mention how it'd be my pleasure. I'm still fucking pissed at the way he treated the woman in my life.

"Go ahead and take me in," he screams at me.

"Ya know what? Turn around, put your hands behind your back."

"For what?"

"Do I really need to count the goddamn reasons?" I push him so that he's facing the wall. "You're violating a protective order, first of all." I press him further into the solid structure, shoving my knee in between his thighs, leaning my weight against him. "Second of all," - I lower my voice, getting closer, speaking low in his ear - "you think you're gonna touch my woman and her not tell me?"

"She's lying," he grunts as I press harder.

"Don't even think about it," I growl. "You say one more word about her, I'll clock out and beat your ass. Not as an officer of the law, but as a man pissed because of what you did to his woman."

"Should you really be bringing your personal feelings into your job, officer?"

"Shut up."

I reach over to my radio, calling for backup. When I'm done, I look over at Montana. "Are you okay? Do you need anyone to come and check you out."

"She's breathing hard, Sully," Leigh says from where she has her arm wrapped around the younger woman. She's handing her a glass of water.

"Probably just scared, but it won't hurt to have someone come and check." I reach back over, keying my radio. "Dispatch go ahead and send an ambulance over to The Café too."

"You okay, deputy?"

"Fine, it's for one of the people involved in the domestic. I'm good and I see back-up pulling in right now."

Ransom comes in, holding Rambo on the leash. His eyes take in the situation. "You straight?"

"Yeah, can you check on her?" I motion over to where Montana sits. "I called for an ambulance. They should be here ASAP."

"Pulling up right now." His gaze watches the street outside The Café. "You taking him in?" He dips his chin at Frank.

"That's the plan."

"He hopes it's the plan," Frank sneers.

"It is, turn around and shut up."

"I see you take her side over mine." He looks at Montana.

"No, you don't look at her," I jerk him around. "You can wait out in the car until we're ready to go."

"I'll be speaking with your supervisor about this."

"Go right ahead." I walk him out, putting him in the back of the car. People gawk as I close the door, thankful I don't have to listen to him any longer. Looking over at the ambulance, I see my sister hop out of the back with her go bag.

"Hey, sis!"

"Hey." She comes over, hugging me around the waist. "How's it going?"

"Pretty quiet day until this piece of shit."

She laughs. "If I had a nickel for every piece of shit both of us have dealt with, we'd be millionaires."

I watch as Rowan goes over, kneeling in front of Montana. Following her, I stand behind, observing. "She was in the hospital until a few days ago because of him." I let her know.

"What happened?" Rowan asks as she takes Montana's blood pressure.

"He beat me," she whispers.

"There's an order of protection against him, and he shouldn't have been here," I answer.

"Your blood pressure is high, which is understandable. Is your chest hurting?"

"Slightly, but I'm starting to calm down some," Montana sighs, taking slow breaths in and out. She leans back against the chair.

"I think you're having an anxiety attack. Let us go put you on the EKG machine for a little while." Ro helps her get up.

"Is he going to jail?"

"Yeah," I tell her.

"Even if I was the one who came here after he did?"

"It doesn't matter where you are or when you walk in. He knows he's supposed to keep his distance from you. If you walk in, he walks out. That's the way it works. None of this is your fault. You need to remember that."

She looks at me, her eyes meeting mine. "I know."

And for the first time I feel like she does. "I'll see y'all later. I'm taking his ass to jail."

CHAPTER 31
SHELBY

"I HADN'T QUITE THOUGHT how I would feel to be up for auction when this idea was presented." I pull at the hem of the dress I'm wearing.

In front of me Sullivan wears a suit, along with a smirk. A fucking smirk. He looks way too good in the white dress shirt, and dark blue blazer. It sets off the color of his eyes, and the perpetual tan he seems to have.

"You look damn good." His gaze eats me up.

"So do you." I grab hold of the lapels of his jacket, tugging him into me. "Wish I had enough money to spend on you. I'm sure you're gonna go for a ton."

I giggle, tilting my head toward him, as he reminds me. "That would be beside the point. Instead of raising money, we'll be spending it."

He slides his hand down my back, cupping my ass with his palm. I grin up at him, loving when a smirk spreads across his face. White teeth flash against his skin. "I'd give everything I had for you."

"Sullivan Baker, you're too sweet."

He dips down, putting his lips to my neck. "Only for you."

Glancing at the clock, I see it's time for us to leave. "We gotta go."

"After you." He ushers me out of the apartment, holding my hand as we head down the stairs to his Mustang.

He opens the passenger side door, grinning like a wolf ready to eat his prey.

I grin back at him, flashing leg as I bend down getting in.

"You do that on purpose," he growls.

"Maybe, maybe not."

"Yeah, you know." He closes the door, a grin on his face.

Crossing my legs, I smile to myself, loving to tease him. He gets in, adjusting his suit pants, before starting the car and putting it in gear.

"Hopefully no crazy MILF bids on you and decides to use you as her hall pass."

He throws his head back, laughing loudly. "You and I've never talked about hall passes. So, I mean, what is your thought about that?"

"I can't believe you're sitting here asking me what I think about hall passes."

He reaches over to grab my hand. "You know I don't want a hall pass."

"But what if she does," I argue.

"I mean we're supposed to give them what they want."

"Well they better not want you."

"When you got it, you got it." He winks.

"You're such a shit, but you're my shit."

"HOW MUCH DO you think Sully will go for?" I ask Stella as we stand to the side of the stage. Stella's not part of the auction, but she's helping with the festivities.

"Sullivan. At least a couple hundred, maybe a thousand."

I gawk at her. "You really think a thousand dollars?"

"You may not realize how hot he is because you see him all the time, but Sully's hot."

"Oh my God, Stelle. This is what I was worried about, some MILF using him for her hall pass."

Stella laughs so hard she wipes tears from her eyes. "You're so salty."

"Well you would be too."

"Oh girl, I already am. You should see the way women look at Ransom when he's out with our kid."

"How do you deal with it?" I ask her, really needing to know how I'm going to ignore the women who stare at our men.

"Every night he comes home to me. I never have to wonder where his affection lies. If we're not together in the morning, he texts to let me know he's thinking about me. When we have time for our lunches together, he surprises me by bringing me food. He, Rambo, and I, we sit on the hood of the SUV and eat as a family. You'll realize it's the little things that count. So many women look at that badge, that gun, and they see the uniform, not the man behind it." She shrugs. "They don't get to see the man who comes home after working a twenty-hour shift. The one who breaks down because there are bad apples in every profession, and it hurts him when things happen on a national level."

I reach out, grabbing Stella's hand because I understand

what she's saying. Even though I've only dealt with it to a smaller degree.

"Or when they come home beat up because a perp or a mentally ill individual put their hands on him. The call, though." She looks down at the ground. "The call is the worst. Where they tell you your boyfriend or husband has been injured in the line of duty. They can't let you know his condition; all you know is you have to get there. Your heart is broken because you're in the dark. No one can prepare you for this, but you have to be strong, Shelby. We love these guys like no one else, and everything that comes with them. You deal with it because you love them. You're their strength and their anchor in a hell of a storm. You ignore the shit thrown at you and you think about how your man makes you feel."

"Sullivan makes me feel amazing." I smirk. "Like I'm the only woman in the world."

"Then that's how you deal with it."

"I got it, Stelle. I understand."

She reaches out, hugging me tightly. "And remember if you ever need people to talk to, you have a whole group of women who know exactly how you feel."

Before I can say anything we hear in the background, "Up next we have Laurel Springs Police Department Officer Sullivan Baker. According to my husband, Tank,"- she gives a smirk - "he enjoys long walks on the beach, candlelight dinners, cuddling with cats, and something about big dick energy."

The room erupts in laughter as Sullivan's face turns a bright, bright shade of red.

The two of us turn our attention to the runway that's

been erected in the building. "God, he looks hot up there," I whisper to Stella as he makes a lap.

"And all these women are seeing it just as much as we are."

Blaze is working the microphone. "We're gonna start out with one hundred dollars, do I hear a hundred?"

"I'd pay five hundred," I whisper.

She cracks up when someone pledges that much. It goes back and forth between Whitney and Leigh.

"Leigh, I know what to do with a younger man," Whitney yells from where she sits. "Eight hundred dollars!"

"Mom!" Stella yells as she turns abruptly to look at her mother. "I can't believe you said that."

"I'm trying to figure out why you're not bidding," she picks up Stella's paddle. "Nine hundred from my daughter."

"She's not interested and we both know it," Leigh raises her paddle. "And if we want to talk about age, I'm younger, Whit, and I can probably keep up with him better. Nine-fifty."

"Ohhhh..." The room groans as the two friends face off.

"Ladies, ladies. There's plenty of me to go around," Sullivan says from the stage.

"No there's not," I yell from where I stand.

Blaze looks back and forth between all of us. She appears to want to be anywhere but here.

"One thousand." Leigh slams her paddle on the table.

"Going once, going twice. Sold to Leigh Thompson for one thousand dollars," Blaze laughs as Leigh shouts in happiness.

"I plan on having him be a waiter for me. Can you imagine the ladies who'll come in to see a man in uniform?"

She claps her hands as she moves up the aisle to pay her donation.

"You coulda asked one of your sons!"

"They're my sons, I wanna at least enjoy the view. With Sully here, I can."

"So you think," Havoc yells from behind the scenes.

The room erupts in laughter at the married couple and I have to admit I feel good knowing she's the woman he's going to be with.

"Your turn." Stella thumbs me up to the stage.

"Wish me luck!"

My body shakes as I stand in front of the room. I've never been one to enjoy being the center of attention, unless I'm in open court.

"We've got one of the best lawyers in the county here folks. Shelby enjoys a good argument, an afternoon Frappuccino, and cinnamon rolls from *A Whole Latte Love*. We'll start it off at one hundred dollars."

The smile is frozen to my face, as I hear people bid on me. My palms sweat as the number continues to go up. I know I won't get the same amount Sully did, but as I get to eight hundred, I'm feeling proud of myself.

"Eight-hundred dollars going once, and twice," Blaze says before she hits her gavel against her podium. "The person who won can come up and claim their prize."

"It was an online bid," Caleb says, where he sits at the back manning a laptop.

Somehow it makes me nervous, but I smile warmly. "Tell them thank you, that money will go a long way."

Turning to the backstage area, I see Sully standing, looking at me. "You ready to get out of here?" he asks.

"You're wearing a dress, and I definitely would love to enjoy it."

"Enjoy it, huh?" I like the sound of that.

"Yeah, I have a little surprise for you."

Sullivan

"KEEP YOUR EYES CLOSED." I reach over covering her line of vision with the blindfold in my hands.

"You're lucky I trust you as much as I do."

"I'm beyond thankful for it." I lean in kissing her neck. "It'll be a couple of hours with this blindfold on, Counselor. You okay with that?"

"How many?"

"A few, you'll see when we get there."

"Okay, Sullivan. I know you're not gonna hurt me." She fumbles as she turns to face me, her lips seeking mine.

For a moment, I give her what she wants before I pull away. "C'mon, get in the car, or we'll never get there. Watch your head." I help her get in, making sure she's buckled in before I close the door.

Jogging around the Mustang, I slide in next to her, a smirk on my face. I can't wait to show Shelby exactly what I have in store for her.

CHAPTER 32
SULLIVAN

"ARE YOU OKAY OVER THERE?" I ask Shelby as we head south on the interstate. She hasn't said much since we left.

"I am." She turns to me, and although I can't see her eyes behind the cloth covering them, I can tell she's sort of irritated I'm keeping her in the dark. "Slightly bored," she huffs. "Thinking about doing something to entertain myself."

"Oh yeah?" I shift gears, getting up to speed to go with the flow of traffic. "What are you planning on doing?"

"I guess I could show you."

The glow from the street lights allow me to see as Shelby sneaks her hand up in between her thighs.

"Oh, Counselor," I groan, putting the car on cruise control. "You horny?"

"For you? Always, but I would love to point out that you were up on that stage lookin' all hot."

"You should've seen yourself, and fun fact, I have a fantasy about you wearing a skirt and letting me fuck you."

She breathes heavily through her nose. "A fantasy?"

"Yeah, one I'm going to make come true when we get to our destination. Tell me what you're doing right now, Shelby."

"Rubbing my finger around my clit."

"Is it enough for you?"

"No," she whines, pressing her hips up.

"Then take your other hand and play with the left nipple. Expose it to my gaze and let me watch as you pluck it."

"Someone could see," she hisses.

"It's dark, it'll only be me."

She moans. "You promise?"

"I do, if anyone else might see, I'll tell you to stop. Make yourself come, Shelby."

She widens her legs, slumping slightly in the seat, allowing her to spread widely. Taking my gaze off the road, I watch as she hitches her skirt up higher, pulls the bra down lower.

"We've only got a few more minutes, Shelby. If you wanna come, you better do it now."

She goes hard after her climax, screaming widely as the blindfold falls from her eyes. She's sucking in air, glancing around. "We're in Birmingham?"

"We are, for the night. I have a bit of a fantasy that I desperately want to make reality."

Together we check in, and go up to the room without bags. Neither one of us packed anything, and I can't bring myself to care.

As we go into the room, I look around for what I specifically asked for.

"Why did you want a table in the middle of the room?" she asks.

"Part of the fantasy. You ready?"

She nods, pulling her lip between her teeth. Grabbing her asscheeks, I hook her legs and take her over to the table. Where I clean it off with one sweep of my arm before bending her over at the waist.

Tits down, ass up.

My breathing becomes labored as I allow myself to have the fantasy I jacked off to so many weeks ago, imagining reaching down, grabbing her skirt and wrenching it up over her cheeks.

There it is. The string of a thong nestled for me to latch onto. Using my fingers, I pull the fabric out, wrapping it around my wrist.

"Sully," she gasps.

"Do you want me to stop?"

Shelby looks over her shoulder at me. Those green eyes of hers hooded with passion. "No." She shakes her head. "Please don't stop."

With my other hand, I tuck my thumb into my palm and extend my middle and index finger as I lift up to her mouth. "Open for me, Counselor."

She accepts my fingers, twirling around them with her tongue, bathing the flesh with moisture that'll ease my way into her body. When I go to extract them, she sucks, refusing to release. "You want something else to suck on?" I breathe into her ear. "I've got it right here for you."

A groan rips from her throat as I move my wet fingers between her thighs, holding them open with my own. I take her in increments. "You're tight." My words are a hiss as I do my best to be patient.

Her head tilts forward as she accepts my invasion, rocking back against my fingers. "Oh my God."

"Yeah?" I crowd into her, getting all up in her personal space. "You like that?"

She nods. "Mmm hmm."

Using my fingers I widen her passage, getting her ready for my length. With my other hand I lift her upper body off the desk, sliding my palm up to her throat, I circle my fingers around the flesh, feeling it move as she swallows roughly. Pulling her neck back, I make a spot big enough for me to move in, open-mouth going after her skin. She squirms as I suck, lick, bite, kiss, and blow against the hot surface, wiggling at my fingers still inside her.

"Sullivan!" she screams, panting, her hands reaching back to grip my thighs tightly. Holding me as close as I can get, until she's coming against my hand, riding it with her head tilted on my shoulder. Inhaling huge gulps of air.

Instead of letting her ease herself down, I quickly push my suit pants and underwear below my dick, grasp my length in my hand for a few seconds and give it a quick jerk before I place it at the opening of her pussy and slide fucking home.

CHAPTER 33
SULLIVAN

A Week Later

"Are you sure there's no one else you want to take with you?" I ask my sister before I practically inhale a drink of the coffee we stopped and picked up. "I'm not sure I'm the person you want to help pick out a wedding dress."

She looks over at me from the driver's seat, a grin on her face. "No one helped me the first time around, and this time, I feel like it's important. You're my best friend."

"But I'm not a girl."

"You don't have to be a girl," she argues. "You more than anyone, know me. You understand what I like and you've been there for me since the beginning."

"But shouldn't you bring Mom or something?"

"If you didn't want to go, you could have said no," she reminds me.

"I know." I take another drink. "I do want to go, but I have to be sure you want me here."

"I invited you!"

"Okay, okay. I'll stop being so self-conscious about it."

"Please do, I'm supposed to be the nervous one."

I give her that, especially after the first marriage she had, she's got to be worried about doing it again. "Are you having second thoughts about getting married."

"There are some days when I worry Cutter's not as great as I've made him out to be in my head. I half-convince myself I've made him into something he's not, but then he does a grand gesture or he just holds me when I need it."

Situating myself in her passenger seat, I mumble slightly. "Is that what women are looking for?"

"If you're asking me about Shelby, then yeah, I know that's what she's looking for. We don't need you to do everything for us, but making us feel safe and wanted? Those are two of the top ways you can show how much you care."

"I hope I make her feel that."

"How are things going with the two of you?"

I think for a second, before smiling. "They're good. Better than."

"Do you see a future with her?"

"Yeah." I take another drink of my coffee. "It won't be quick like yours and Cutter's. She wants to get her practice off the ground, but I see a future with her."

"Like a house and two point five kids future?"

Used to be that scared me, but thinking about it with Shelby? It's not as scary as it once was. In fact, I do see the house and kids. "Yeah, yeah, I see that with her."

"Oh my God, Sully. Have you told her?"

"No, not yet."

"What the hell are you waiting for?"

"The right time?"

"There will never be a right time, Sullivan. You know

that as well as I do. If you wait until *the right time*, you may be waiting forever."

While I know she's telling the truth, it's still scary to put my heart out there for anyone. Especially after what happened the last time I put myself on the line. "I'm working up to it," I say, trying to defend my actions.

"You better hope no one else is working up to it while you are."

My heart rate spikes. "Do you know something I don't?"

"No," she laughs. "I'm just saying, how long is she going to wait?"

"It's not like we've been together for years, Rowan. Jesus. Shut the hell up."

"This is my day," she retorts. "*You* shut the hell up."

I hold up my hands in surrender. "Then you tell me what you want me to do. Just don't bring up my relationship with Shelby. I'm figuring out what I want to do."

"Don't take forever, big bro. We're here."

Sighing, I see what looks like some sort of boutique.

"Oh suck it up big guy, you get to see me get all pretty."

I saw it once before, but she never had the spark in her eye she has now. There was no smile she now wears constantly, and I never trusted her first husband the way I do Cutter. "C'mon, Cinderella, let's go find your dress."

I hold out my arm to her, and together we walk into the building. We enter, and are greeted immediately.

"Hi, I'm Rowan Baker, I called earlier this week about seeing a few dresses."

"Hello." The girl shakes her hand. "I'm Bridget, I'm the one who spoke with you. Is this your fiancé?"

"No," she laughs looking at me. "This is my older

brother. I trust him and he's come to help me choose my dress."

"Well we're excited to have you here. I've pulled the dresses you indicated you're interested in. This dressing room is yours." She leads Rowan to what looks like a woman's dream. It's pink and white with quilted walls and other delicate-looking features.

"If you wanna sit there." She points to a chair outside the room. "We'll get her ready, and bring her out to show you. Would you like something to drink?"

"Water, please."

One of the workers comes over, giving me a cold bottle. "Do you have any questions?" she asks as she hands it to me.

"How many dresses does she have back there?"

"Trying to figure out how long you'll be here?" She gives a knowing look.

"Slightly."

"From what I can see," - she lifts an iPad up - "she has five dresses. If she picks one of those it shouldn't be more than a couple of hours."

"And if not?"

"Good luck, buddy."

I laugh, running a hand through my shaggy hair, a smile on my face. No matter how much I act like this is annoying to me, I love that Rowan invited me.

The woman who greeted us when we came in, peeks out. "She looks beautiful. You ready to see?"

"Yup." I nod, sitting forward with my elbows on my knees, clasping my fingers together.

The door opens all the way and the person who walks out can't be Rowan. This woman looks like she's stepped out of the pages of one of those wedding magazines. In front of my eyes, Rowan has gone from my little sister to a woman who looks like she has all the confidence in the world.

She comes out, twirling. I'm sure the lights are supposed to make the dress twinkle and sparkle like someone's thrown pixie dust on her. The smile on her face is as wide as I've ever seen.

"You look absolutely beautiful, Rowan. Like all your dreams as a kid when you wanted to be a princess have come to life. Don't even try the rest of them on." I grab my phone out and take a picture. "This is it, Ro."

"It is, isn't it?" She clasps her hands in front of her, cheese-smiling as she comes closer to me.

"It is." I show her the picture I took. "Looks like it was made for you."

She grabs hold of my phone, grinning at herself. "It's definitely the one. They didn't even have to adjust it, at all. It's perfect."

"Which is unheard of," the saleswoman says to us. "Would you like to try some more on, or is this it?"

Rowan turns, lifting up the skirt, moving over to a platform that allows her to view herself in the round. There, with all the lights around her, she appears to be on her own red carpet, camera bulbs flashing to capture her happiness.

"Yes." She turns to all of us. "This is it."

The saleswoman helps her back into the room, presumably to get her out of the dress. I finish drinking the bottle of water they gave me before she gets out. Rowan is beaming as she comes out. "I love it, and I'm so thankful you were here with me to see it."

"I don't think you needed me to know that dress was for you."

"Yeah I did." She hugs me close.

"Okay, Ms. Baker, per the contract, we'll measure you two weeks before your wedding, and make sure everything still fits. Are you wanting to pay a down payment today, and do payments on the remaining balance?"

I'm barely paying attention to what they're talking about until I hear them say fifteen hundred down and then a remaining amount of four thousand dollars. I want to do a double-take, but I try to keep it in, until she's done.

We walk out together, and after the door shuts, I turn to her. "That damn thing was almost six thousand dollars?"

"Wedding dresses are expensive, Sully. You better get used to it for when Shelby wants one." She elbows me in the side. "I know, I know, don't rush you. But seriously, Dad's paying for the remaining balance on it. He didn't approve of my first marriage, and he more than approves of this one. He and Cutter have a great relationship. This is his gift to us."

"Well, that's gonna make my gift look like shit."

She stops and hugs me tight. "My gift from you is that you always have my back, no matter what the situation, and there can never be a price put on that."

CHAPTER 34
SHELBY

I'LL BE glad when this shit is over and I'll never volunteer for anything like this with the LSERT again. I'd been led to believe there wouldn't be anyone not vetted, but I guess money is money. Something told me not to do this, but I'm the new one here and I wanna help all my new friends. I've had a shitty feeling about this since I got the directions to the dinner tonight. All of our correspondence has been done by email. To be honest, I wanted to get this over with, so I agreed to meet them on the first day they requested.

It's not in a part of Laurel Springs I've ever been in, and I don't recall there being a restaurant in the building I've been directed to, but I gave my word and here I am.

"I'm here," I tell Rowan. "If you don't hear from me in an hour, send help," I half-way joke. "I know this is supposed to be a new place, but it doesn't look open."

"Be careful."

As I get out of my car, I lock the doors and make sure the pepper spray I like to carry is within easy reach. Slowly I walk up to the front entrance, knocking on the door.

Glancing in through the glass, I see that work has been done, but this place isn't ready to be open for business yet. That bad feeling I had comes back with a vengeance.

Head down, I'm walking back to my car when I feel something grab around my neck. Immediately I go to scream, but a hand clamps over my mouth.

"Hey, Shelby, you ready for a wonderful time together?"

I would know that voice anywhere. Frank Gentry.

Fear radiates all through my body as I immediately begin trying to think of ways to get out of this situation. In Houston I'd taken self-defense courses, but since I've moved, I haven't kept up with them. Instead of instinctively knowing what to do, I know without a doubt, I'm fighting for my life.

I pick my foot up, slamming it down onto Frank's. He howls, letting go of my mouth, which allows me to use my teeth to bite him. Taking off, I run for my car.

"You fucking bitch! You will pay for what you took away from me."

I can hear him behind me. He's taller and faster. All I want to do is get to my car, lock the doors, and try to drive away. I'm close when I feel his fingers in my hair, yanking against the strands, pushing my face down into the concrete.

Screaming wildly, I turn over, scratching at his eyes, his cheeks, anything I can reach. A blow rocks my head. We fight against one another, me clawing for the pepper spray I made sure was close enough to grab. When I tighten my fingers around it, I pull it out, pressing against the button, aiming at his eyes.

"You whore, you won't get away with this!"

Scrambling to my feet, I rush to my car, opening the door, but Frank grabs hold of my purse. He's reaching in, trying to get the keys. Somehow I wrestle them out of his hands, and I know immediately I won't be able to keep him at bay for much longer. There's only one thing for me to do, in order to buy myself enough time. I use the key fob to unlock the door, and then as he lunges for me, I throw it, as fucking far as I can.

"You stupid idiot!" He turns, watching for where it lands.

I have just enough time to get in and lock the doors. Fumbling with my cell phone, managing to dial nine-one-one right as he starts beating on the windows.

"Help me! Help me!" I scream into the phone, yelling out the address.

I don't know where he gets it from, but a rock comes through the driver's side window and he yanks the phone out of my hand, throwing it in the same direction as my keys. "What are you doing?"

His fingers tangle in my hair, pulling me out of the car. "Teaching you what it feels like to be helpless."

Sullivan

THE MID-AFTERNOON into evening so far has been quiet, which is typically a death-sentence for the end of shift. Glancing at the clock on my dashboard, it reads six-thirty.

Thirty minutes.

Then I can go home, get out of these clothes, and wait for Shelby to get back from her dinner. She was supposed to text me when she got there, but I haven't gotten one yet. When I stop at the next red light I hit, I'll give her a call to make sure she's good.

As I brake to a stop and grab my cell phone, dispatch comes over the radio.

"Nine-one-one hang up from a cell phone. GPS shows it's over in the new warehouse district. Emergency services tried to call back and there's no answer. They heard screaming in the background."

I'm three minutes from the location. "Mark me as responding. I'll be there ASAP."

Flipping on my lights and pressing the gas pedal sends my adrenaline rushing. My tires squeal, and I grip the steering wheel as the engine responds. Turning onto the street, my pulse increases because the car sitting there looks like Shelby's.

There's a man pulling a blonde woman out of the driver's side window. My lights illuminate them, I'd recognize that motherfucker Frank Gentry anywhere.

Squealing to a stop, I get out, holding my gun on him. "Hands up!"

"Who are you gonna pick, Sullivan? Your woman, or me?"

She screams when he pulls her hair, dragging her through the window.

"Let her go!"

"Make a decision, Sullivan."

"Let her go." My voice is hoarse, desperation making me willing to do anything he wants me to.

He yanks on her harder, dropping her on the asphalt. The groan that escapes her throat is pitiful. My eyes and his lock; he knows I'm going to choose her. I'll always choose her.

Before I can holster my gun, I take a shot at him, but I

know it's going to miss. My attention isn't on him, it's completely on her.

"Shelby!"

She's bleeding and her eyes aren't open. Fumbling with my radio, I manage to put words to what is happening. "Dispatch, I need an ambulance. Suspect is on the loose, it's Frank Gentry. Shelby Bruce is the victim," I choke out.

"Sullivan, they'll have someone there as soon as possible."

Everyone knows how much this woman means to me. Throwing my radio down, I reach out to check her over. "Shelby, can you hear me?" She groans as I push the hair from her forehead. There's blood everywhere, and I don't know what to do first.

"How far away are they?" I scream into my radio. "She's not conscious."

"They'll be there within minutes," dispatch assures me.

My fear is it won't be in enough time.

"Hang on for me, Counselor." I cradle her head in my lap. "I love you." My voice is hoarse and I feel uncharacteristic tears pool in my eyes, begging the ambulance to hurry up.

CHAPTER 35
SULLIVAN

"WHERE IS SHELBY?" Menace asks as I stride back into headquarters, going to the equipment room to load up on what I feel I need.

"She's at the hospital. They're going to keep her overnight. Concussion."

I don't want to speak to him or anyone else. There's only one thing on my mind and that's finding Frank.

"Then why aren't you there with her?" Menace questions.

"I have other things to do."

"You don't want to do this." He grabs hold of my shoulder, stopping me from going any farther.

"You have no idea what I'm about to do." I throw his hand off me.

"No, I do." He grabs hold and pushes me back against the wall. "I know exactly how you feel. When Rina was pregnant with Kels, she was held at gunpoint by a fellow teacher. I wanted to run in there and grab her, make sure she was okay, kill the fucker with my bare hands. But I couldn't."

He holds onto my arm. "I had to be off the case, I was too close. In my anger I wanted to go in there and kill everyone, which wouldn't have done shit for what really needed to happen. I'm telling you as a man who understands your emotions right now, you need to go to the hospital and stay with her."

I shake my head. "You didn't see what she looked like. Blood pouring from her cheek, glass everywhere, bruises all over her face. I can't let him go and not get retribution."

"He will get it," Menace vows. "But it can't come from you, Sully. It cannot come from you. Trust us to take care of you. To avenge whatever you need us to. Go to the hospital and be with Shelby."

Sighing, I have to admit I understand what he's saying, but at the same time I hate it. "If I do anything, I'll be charged?"

"You will."

That's all I have to hear. My identity is a police officer, I can't be one if I'm charged. In order to be the best man I can for Shelby, I need to be who I am. And above all I'm an officer of the law.

"HOW IS SHE?" I ask my sister as I enter Shelby's hospital room.

Rowan responded to the call, thank God, because I'm not sure I would've been able to be patient with anyone else while they helped her.

"She hasn't woken up yet, but she's responsive when they do tests. Everyone thinks she should come around soon."

I walk over to the other side of her bed, having a seat in the chair. Her face is bruised, purple and blue standing out in stark relief against the fair color of her skin. "Counselor, I'm so sorry."

"This wasn't your fault," Rowan says softly.

"It was, I should've known he'd do something like this. He was fucking escalating."

"No one could have known. You aren't a super hero."

"I'm not, but I keep my family safe, and I couldn't do it for her." Reaching over, I grab hold of her hand, squeezing it tightly.

"I knew you would come." I hear Shelby croak out. "While I was lying there, I kept telling myself you would come."

"Shhh." I push her hair back from her face. "Don't say anything. You need to save your strength."

"Did you catch him?"

"I didn't, but they've sent a team to hunt him. They wouldn't allow me to be part of it. I shot at him, but I missed. I was more worried about you."

"You should never think about me before your safety."

"Without you, my safety doesn't fuckin' matter, Counselor."

She moans when she turns her head.

"Are you okay?"

"It hurts."

"You have a concussion," Rowan explains. "Let me go get the doctor on call to give you some more medicine."

When Rowan leaves, Shelby looks up at me. "I promised myself while I was lying there, I would tell you if I had the chance. I love you, Sully. I love you so much I almost can't breathe for it."

Running my finger down her cheek, I lean in, kissing her softly. "Love you too, Shelby. I've never been so scared in my life, and fair warning, I'll never let you out of my sight again."

She cries softly. "I'm perfectly fine with that."

The doctor comes in, and I reluctantly remove myself from beside her, but I know without a doubt that's one promise I'll keep to my death.

TWO HOURS LATER, Cruise comes in wearing his SWAT gear, his gun on his thigh, black soot on his face.

"Did you get him?"

He shakes his head. "Frank Gentry burnt his house down. He was DOA. We just brought his body in."

Shelby makes a noise in her throat. "I can't say I'm sorry, but even though he was an ass to Montana, it's gonna hurt. She lived with him for a long time. Can someone go tell her?"

"I will," Cruise says. "It's the least I can do. I'm sorry you got caught in the middle of this, Shelby."

"I always knew it could happen. Thanks for making sure he won't be hurting anyone else."

"Yeah." I hold out my hand for him to shake. "Thanks for taking care of it for me."

"With pleasure my brother, you take care of her."

"Trust me, I will." I have a seat next to her, and vow right now to make sure she's safe for the rest of her life.

CHAPTER 36
SHELBY

"THIS IS THE CAFÉ," I tell my parents as we make the trip down the sidewalk from my office to the place where most people in town go to eat. They've been here for almost two weeks. Since I was brought to the hospital and now that I'm home.

They leave tomorrow, and I finally feel well enough to take them on a tour of Laurel Springs.

"It's all so quaint." My mom grins. "I can see why you love this place."

"It's not hard," I admit.

We walk in being greeted by so many people who have become friends and family to me in such a short amount of time. Seeing three swivel chairs at the soda fountain free, I lead them to my favorite place to sit. That's when I notice Ransom, Cruise, and Havoc standing in a group together, cracking up.

"Hey guys." I wave. "What's going on?"

Ransom giggles as he looks at me. "Your man is in a slow speed chase."

"Slow speed chase?" I ask, not sure what he's saying. I'm not sure I've ever heard of a slow speed chase.

"Mr. Honeycutt is refusing to pull over. Apparently Sully has it out for him because he got in the way of a call. He ran Honeycutt's license and it hasn't been renewed since seventy-fuckin'-nine."

I can't help but giggle. "So he's got a vendetta against a ninety-five year old man?"

"How fast are you going?" dispatch asks.

"Twenty-five." I can hear Sullivan say over the radio, sirens blaring.

"Tell him to let it go." I roll my eyes.

Caleb, who is on shift, keys his radio. "Your girlfriend says let it go, Baker."

"He's breaking the law," he argues.

"Give me the radio." I move my fingers in a gimme motion. "How does this thing work?"

Caleb shows me how to get on, and I shake my head before speaking. "I swear to God, Sully. You arrest him, I'll have him out in ten minutes. Let him go. He's lived his life."

"Why are you on the radio?"

"Because this is stupid," I laugh.

"I'll show you stupid."

We hear sirens as they come to a stop outside The Café. Turning around, I watch as Sully turns his car off, and gets out, holding a bouquet of flowers in his hands.

A smirk plays against the edges of my lips as I watch him stroll in, oblivious to all the eyes looking him up and down. "Is that what's stupid?" I raise an eyebrow at the flowers.

"No." He shakes his head. "I'm the one who's stupid. Just wanted to let you know I've got a good thing, and I'm gonna keep it."

Tears fill my eyes before glancing over at my parents. "As you can see, I'm well taken care of here."

Dad stands up to shake Sullivan's hand, before turning to face me. "That's all we ever wanted for you, Shelby, and. I think we both agree," - he looks back at Mom - "this is your home now."

I nod, launching myself at Sullivan. Best news I've heard all day.

CHAPTER 37
SULLIVAN

"I LOVE that shirt almost as much as I love you." I wrap my arms tightly around Shelby's waist. Since she came home from the hospital, I've had her within my reach.

She wrinkles her nose up cutely at me. "I have no idea why."

"Oh you know." I turn her around in my arms.

The front of it says *Laurel Springs SWAT Team* and on the back it says *Baker*. One day I'll make her last name the same as mine. We're in no hurry. For the first time in my life, I'm not in a hurry.

To prove to my family how much better I am than my brother.

To do what everyone thinks I should be doing.

Finally, I'm becoming my own man.

"You gonna be there at the end?"

"Oh yeah, hooting and hollering for the hottest guy on the course."

I smile, shaking my head. "You're good for my ego."

She reaches up, running her fingers through my hair. "You're good for me period."

"So if we win, does that mean I get to do whatever I want to you?" I rub my nose against her neck.

"I believe you said something about cooking with nothing but an apron on."

"I did." I clasp my arms around her.

Since we moved in together a month ago, we've had a lot of fun interludes. She winks. "Then you better get busy and win."

I kiss her quickly. "Wish me luck."

"Good luck, Sully."

"Let's go!" Ransom yells, whistling to get everyone's attention. "It's time for us to sign in."

Shelby smacks my ass. "Go get me a W."

"Will do, babe."

Shelby

"LOOK AT HIM." I grab hold of Stella's shirt. "Walking with that gun like he owns the place."

"There's something about the swagger of these guys. All long-legged, full of cockiness, and so fuckin' hot."

Kels joins us. "Yes, yes they do. We're some lucky bitches. To have those men in our beds at night."

"And our kitchens during the day." I wink.

"Look at you," Stella laughs. "Just wait until you have kids, there will be no more fucking on the kitchen table."

"Wasn't exactly the kitchen table, more like the chair."

They giggle as we watch the guys do the individual events, along with the team ones.

"They just pulled into the lead." Rina whistles, clapping loudly. "My husband may not be on that team, but my son is," she explains to anyone who looks around.

Glancing up at the leaderboard I see they're in the number one spot. Calvert City in second and Paradise Lost in third.

"Let's go, Laurel!" We clap as we come up to the last event. It's a foot race, but set up like a relay. Each man wearing all their gear.

"Let's go, Laurel!"

Clap, clap, clap-clap-clap.

"Let's go, Laurel!"

"Fuck," Rowan groans from where she stands next to me. "Sully's going against our brother."

I have yet to meet Braylon, but I will tonight at the family dinner that's been planned. Looking further down the track they've set up, I see the two of them standing next to each other. I'd know Sullivan anywhere, but the man standing beside him would look familiar in a crowd.

They look to be close to the same height, but Sullivan is taller, and a bit more muscular. That hair of his hanging in his eyes is the sexiest thing I've seen. Especially since I know it's wet with the sweat of hard work.

Paradise Lost is slightly ahead as Braylon is passed on the baton, taking off quickly.

"C'mon, Laurel Springs!" I scream, stamping my feet on the bleachers we're sitting in.

After what feels like a year, Sully grabs hold of the baton and my man takes off like a shot. His long legs eat up the distance between him and his brother.

"C'mon baby!" I yell. "You got this!"

He's close to his brother, so close I can't tell the difference between the two of them anymore. He's breathing down his neck. Rowan sits next to me, her fingers clasped tightly over her mouth. I can tell she doesn't want to cheer for either of them. She's in a bad spot.

"It's okay, I'll cheer loud enough for the both of us."

She grins, and we start jumping up and down, as they get closer to us.

"C'mon, Sully!"

When they get right in front of us, I pick the perfect moment. "If you want that apron, you better run!"

He hears me, and he kicks it into high gear, crossing the finish line right before his brother. The crowd erupts in hoots, howls, and screams. We're all down the bleachers within a few seconds.

I take off at a run, throwing myself into Sullivan's arms, wrapping my legs around his waist. His strong grip holds me tightly.

"You won!"

"I did," he gasps out his breath. "I won."

Someone comes up behind us, but he doesn't put me down.

"Good game, bro."

I try to disentangle myself from him, but Sullivan refuses to let loose. "You too." He holds me with one hand. I feel him offer his other out to his brother.

"This the woman who finally got you?" a female voice speaks.

This time he does let me down.

"Candice, I'd like to introduce you to Shelby Bruce." He sneaks his arm around my neck. I lean into him, not caring about the sweat sticking to his skin.

"Nice to meet you," she says.

I notice her and Braylon don't stand together like we do. Maybe they aren't as happy as they'd like people to believe.

"Nice to meet you too. I do have to thank you." I look up at Sully, kissing his jawline.

"Thank me?"

"You let this one go, so I could scoop him up. Your loss, but he's the best luck I ever had."

Rowan snorts from behind us, and Sullivan chuckles. "C'mon, Counselor, let's go get some water."

"With pleasure." I hug him tightly, letting him lead me over to the refreshment table.

"Have I told you how much I love you?" he asks after he gulps a bottle of water.

"I think I know."

"You can't know." He tucks his hands in the back pockets of my jeans. "Because no one's ever stood up for me with my brother the way you just did."

"It's my pleasure," I purr into his ear.

"What's gonna be my pleasure is seeing these bare-asscheeks bending over as they make me double-chocolate brownies."

I laugh, not able to ignore the heat between my thighs.

"You want it tonight?" I ask as I move back, biting my lip.

"Yes. Every. Single. Night."

This man?

Those words?

Best I've ever heard.

EPILOGUE ONE
SULLIVAN

My heart swells in my chest as Rowan walks down the aisle toward the man who will be her husband. Standing in front of the church, along with the man who she'll give herself to, I swallow hard. The dress I helped her pick out looks incredible as it sparkles in the candlelight of the chapel.

As much as I thought she was beautiful then, she's gorgeous now. The wide smile across her face, the wetness in her eyes, and the sparkle that radiates from inside competes with the one she wears on the outside.

Our dad is like the rest of us in our dress uniforms. Even though he and I don't always see eye-to-eye, I'm still proud of the awards he wears on his chest.

As they step to the altar, Cutter comes down, holding out his hand for Rowan.

"Who gives this woman to this man?"

"Her family and I do," Dad answers, before kissing Rowan on the cheek and heading over to where Mom sits.

She wipes at her eyes, which means she's crying. Mom always cries at important moments in her kids' lives.

"We are gathered here today..." the preacher starts, and as I listen, I look across the way. My eyes connect with the love of my life.

Shelby smiles softly at me, and I answer it back with one of my own.

The two of us have grown closer since Frank killed himself. It's a wonder I ever let her out of my sight, but I've learned to trust her. She got herself out of the situation as best she could, and then I cleaned it up. Together we've worked through the nightmares and fear.

"I now pronounce you husband and wife. Cutter, you may now kiss your bride."

We watch them go down the aisle, and then we start pairing up with our bridesmaids to make our way out of the chapel. I come together with Shelby, holding my arm out to her.

"You look beautiful."

"You're not so bad yourself," she sasses back.

For hours we pose with the rest of our friends, taking wedding picture after wedding picture. I don't mind though, because I'm with Shelby.

"It's been a great day," Shelby whispers as we dance later at the reception. Her arms are around my neck and we're swaying to a slow beat.

"Can you see this being us one day?"

She puts her head on my shoulder. "I can, but only when it's the right time."

"So you're in no hurry?"

She shakes her head. "Not at all, I'm ready for whatever you're ready for."

"Come with me?"

"You know I'll follow you wherever you go."

EPILOGUE ONE

Grabbing her hand, we dash through the crowd out to the balcony. It's lit up with soft outdoor bulbs, a couple of drinking stations, and what will later on be a packed dance floor. Walking her over to the ledge, we face one another.

"You look beautiful." I grasp her chin with my forefinger and thumb. "My mind kept wondering throughout the ceremony."

"Wondering about what?" She beams up at me.

"It kept thinking how much I adore you." I bend down, capturing her lips with mine.

"Sully." The name comes out on a whisper before they touch.

It's a slow possession, one filled with passion and promise. I'm careful to not let it get out of hand. "I have something for you."

"Do you?" She lifts her eyebrows up in question.

"Yeah." I grin. "You know you've become my best friend, right? I hate sleeping without you, I don't do well if you aren't around to wish me a good shift, if possible, I wanna have my lunch and dinner with you. Breakfast too." She laughs when I add on that little tidbit. "But what I want more than anything is to make that shirt you wear when I'm having SWAT events come true."

"What?"

I reach into my suit pocket. "When you wear that jersey with the name Baker on it. I want that to be true, Counselor. You're already my family, but I want to make it official."

Bending down on one knee, I open the box to the ring that screamed her when I first saw it. "Shelby, will you marry me?"

Her hand covers her mouth, her green eyes sparkling in the night with unshed tears. "It's beautiful."

"As beautiful as you are." My voice shakes as I wait for her to answer. "It's morganite," I ramble. "Learned a lot when I was searching for the best for you."

"Sullivan Baker, you are the best man I've ever known. I love you more than I thought possible. Yes, Sully, yes!"

Launching off the ground, I wrap her tightly in my arms, twirling her around. And while we spin, I see the entire reception is watching us through the windows.

"She said yes!" I yell.

The group erupts, family and friends coming out to congratulate us, and as I look across the balcony, locking eyes with the woman of my dreams, I know our future is going to be everything we've always wanted. And everything Shelby Bruce deserves.

EPILOGUE TWO
DEVANTE

As has become my habit when I'm working the morning shift, I park the ambulance in front of *A Whole Latte Love*. "You want anything?" I ask Cutter who's feverishly texting. Ten bucks says it's to his brand-new wife, Rowan.
"Black, one cream, two sugars."
"Then it's not black, is it?"
"Don't give me shit this morning. Ro gained two pounds and she's convinced she won't be able to fit into any of her clothes now. Never mind we've already gotten married."
"This is why you got married, and not me," I remind him. Marriage isn't my deal. Never has been, probably never will be.
"I'm gonna call her, try and talk her down from the damn ledge."
"Good luck with that my man."
Gratefully, I leave him in the ambulance by himself. I might be happy for him, but he's driven me crazy talking about this wedding the last few months. Walking into the

coffee shop, I expect to see Eden at the counter with a smile on her face.

That's how I've seen her almost every day since she opened. Today though, it's different. "Eden," I yell out, expecting her to come from the back.

When she doesn't, I decide to go do a little searching for her. Something isn't sitting right with me, and there's a tingle in the pit of my stomach telling me to find her. Going behind the counter, I enter the cooking area, and that's where I see her. She's sitting down, bent over at the waist. "Are you okay?"

Brown eyes full of pain meet mine. "I feel like a have a knot in the middle of my chest." She shifts around. "I haven't been able to get comfortable for the past few days. My back is killing me."

One of the things I've taken to doing is carrying my stethoscope with me. Walking over to her, I have her lean back. "Deep breath." She can barely do what I'm asking, but I can hear movement in her digestive track. I've seen this more than once. "Do you have your gallbladder?"

"Yeah." She tips her head back, grabbing hold of my hand. "My God, the pain just keeps coming in waves."

"C'mon." I pull her up from where she sits. "We need to get you to the hospital."

"Devante, no." She tries to fight against the pull. "There's no way I can close the shop. I'm barely making it, as is."

"Listen to me." I grab her cheeks with my hands. "If you're as sick as I think you are, you're gonna need surgery. You mess around with this? You can get sepsis and then it won't matter, Eden." There's a fear I don't like to see in her eyes.

Tears spring, and I want nothing more than to tell her everything is going to be okay. Unfortunately, I'm not a doctor, and I don't know it for sure. "Okay." She wipes at the tears. "Let's go."

Slowly, we walk toward the ambulance and as soon as Cutter sees us, he gets out, running over. "What's happening?"

"I think it's her gallbladder."

"We need to lock the doors," she protests.

"Oh my God, Eden. Are you okay?" Shelby yells as she pulls up and gets out of her car.

"I'm sick." Her voice is pitiful.

"Sick enough that I'm taking her to the hospital," I interject.

"Shelby," her tone begs, "as a small business owner, I can't stand to not have a day of sales."

"I get you." She reaches over, grabbing her hand. "I can't cook, but I'll figure out how to run the cash register."

"Things are already made up, and there are directions on how to prepare it. Please just keep it open as long as you can."

"I'll help too." I hear Leigh's voice chime in.

"You have your own restaurant to run," Eden protests.

"And I have so many people I can call in to help both of us. Don't you worry, we'll make sure you're taken care of."

"Are they for real?" she asks, looking at me.

"They are. There's one thing you'll learn about this town. They love to help their own."

"I'm not one of their own," she cries.

Grabbing her hand, I put it against my chest. "You are now, trust me. You are now."

Preorder Devante - LSERT #6 November 5th, 2021

ABOUT THE AUTHOR

Laramie Briscoe is the USA Today and Wall Street Journal Bestselling Author of over 30 books.

Since self-publishing her first book in May of 2013, Laramie has appeared on the Top 100 Bestselling E-books Lists on Amazon Kindle, Apple Books, Barnes & Noble, and Kobo. Her books have been known to make readers laugh and cry. They are guaranteed to be emotional, steamy reads.

When she's not writing alpha males who seriously love their women, she loves spending time with friends, reading, and marathoning shows on Netflix. Married to her high school sweetheart, Laramie lives in Bowling Green, KY with her husband (the Travel Coordinator) and a sometimes crazy cat named Beau.

facebook.com/authorlaramiebriscoe
twitter.com/laramiebriscoe
instagram.com/laramie_briscoe
bookbub.com/authors/laramie-briscoe

REPORT ERRORS/REVIEWS

LEAVE A REVIEW

IF THERE WAS a part you loved of "Sullivan", please don't hesitate to leave a review and let other readers know!

If you do leave a review, please email me with the link so that I can say a personal 'thank you'!!! They mean a lot, and I want to let you know I appreciate you taking the time out of your day!

Email Me

REPORT AN ERROR

Also, if you find an error, know that it has slipped through no less than four sets of eyes, and it is a mistake. Please let me know, if you find one, and if I agree it's an error. It will be changed. Thank you!

Report Errors

CONNECT WITH LARAMIE

Patreon:
patreon.com/laramiebriscoe
Website:
www.laramiebriscoe.net
Facebook:
facebook.com/AuthorLaramieBriscoe
Twitter:
twitter.com/LaramieBriscoe
Pinterest:
pinterest.com/laramiebriscoe
Instagram:
instagram.com/laramie_briscoe
Mailing List:
http://sitel.ink/LBList
Email:
laramie@laramiebriscoe.com

ALSO BY LARAMIE BRISCOE

The Haldonia Monarchy

Royal Rebel

Royal Chaos

Royal Love

Heaven Hill Series

Meant To Be

Out of Darkness

Losing Control

Worth The Battle

Dirty Little Secret

Second Chance Love

Rough Patch

Beginning of Forever

Home Free

Shield My Heart

A Heaven Hill Christmas

Heaven Hill Next Generation

Hurricane

Wild

Fury

Hollow

Heaven Hill Shorts

Caelin

Christine

Justice

Harley

Jagger

Charity

Liam

Drew

Dalton

Mandy

Rockin' Country Series

Only The Beginning

The Price of Love

Full Circle

Hard To Love

Reaper's Love

The Nashvegas Trilogy

Power Couple

Breach of Contract

The Moonshine Task Force Series

Renegade

Tank

Havoc

Ace

Menace

Cruise

Laurel Springs Emergency Response Team

Ransom

Suppression

Enigma

Cutter

Sullivan

The MVP Duet

On the DL

MVP

The Midnight Cove Series

Inflame

Stand Alones

My Confession

Sketch

Sass

Trick

Room 143

2018 Laramie Briscoe Compilation

2019 Laramie Briscoe Compilation

Made in the USA
Columbia, SC
16 July 2023